House of Dagger

Julian R Hillis

ISBN:9798816010993

DEDICATION

This book is dedicated to all my readers, like you.

Thank you.

CONTENTS

Acknowledgements

00- Prologue - 1

01 - Chapter One - 7

02 - Chapter Two - 13

03 - Chapter Three - 19

04 - Chapter Four - 26

05 - Chapter Five - 32

06 - Chapter Six - 39

07 - Chapter Seven - 46

08 - Chapter Eight - 52

09 - Chapter Nine - 59

10 - Chapter Ten - 67

11 - Chapter Eleven - 73

12 - Chapter Twelve - 80

13 - Chapter Thirteen - 89

14 - Chapter Fourteen - 99

15 - Chapter Fifteen - 106

16 - Chapter Sixteen - 114

17 - Chapter Seventeen - 121

18 - Chapter Eighteen - 128

19 - Chapter Nineteen - 136

20 - Chapter Twenty - 142

ACKNOWLEDGMENTS

Words don't even begin to cover how all this wouldn't be possible without my loving partner. She is my rock, my emotional support. Thank you for everything you do.

And to my mother, the one woman who, from the very first story, saw potential in me. You grew and nurtured my love of reading and writing from a very young age. You taught me that no idea is a bad one.

00 - Prologue -

His mate, Inn. DEAD.

How could he carry on? They were not the traditional mates, but they had grown to be friends at least? The paper he held in his hands, the death certificate. It claimed Inn died in childbirth, but how could Inn have died in such a way? They had never had sex; they didn't even sleep in the same room. That meant Inn had been sleeping outside of their marriage and that hurt a little, but not as bad as losing Inn hurt.

Skorwn males that could birth their own children were very rare and often died in the birth. It was like a one in fifty thousand chance a male could carry. He wondered if Inn's child had made it into the world alive, what would become of

Inn's child? The death of Inn would remove Dagger from the House of Prodigy. If the child had been his, it would have allowed him to keep the position in the first family, but that was not the case. His rank drop was not even that much. Dagger belonged to the House of White. That meant his bloodline was the second to form the second family. Not like that was of any importance right now. The important thing was about what they would do with his husband and the child. Whether dead or alive.

Somewhere in a back room, the male, Prodigy, screamed in anger. His sweet son, Inn. Died in childbirth. The blond tuffs on the head of Inn's son told him alone, Inn's husband, Dagger, was not this child's father. Inn had broken his marriage and bore a child. This was bad, all kinds of bad. Not just because he had been the one to set Inn and Dagger for marriage, but because it had been his son that broke the marriage vows. That would make his family look bad.

Prodigy did not know what to do with this child at this point. Well, Prodigy and Dagger did not see eye to eye, he was not angry when the doctor presented him with the audio from the childbirth. Inn's voice rang out from the tape, loud and clear. It made his blood boil with a feeling he had never felt.

Please make sure my son goes to Dagger. He must.

Prodigy would take the child to Dagger the moment they cleared it to leave. The birth certificate in his hand named the child as Wick, Son of Inn, House of Prodigy.

Prodigy saw nothing he was not pleased with other than they listed him under the house of Prodigy, well this was his grandchild. He did not belong under the house of Prodigy, but that would change once Dagger took the child. He would be Wick, Son Of Inn, House of Dagger. Prodigy was not the one who should be listed on the birth certificate. It disgusted him they had done that.

Once the child had been cleared, Prodigy took the infant to Dagger. He didn't knock as he walked inside the home his son once lived. Prodigy was met at the entranceway by Dagger, Son of Risk.

"Inn named you guardian of his child, Wick, son of Inn."

Dagger looked at the small infant and couldn't believe his ears. The child he had worried about was here in his home. Inn had named him the Guardian. Just why the hell had Inn done that? Wick had a father, and it was not him.

"Why I? Why not the child's father?"

"Inn didn't have any father present or on the birth certificate. He had also demanded before he passed that you be the one to have the child, that you must take him. He wanted no one else to have the infant."

"I see. But I still really don't understand why he would want me to have the infant. But I will look after the infant."

He passed over the tiny infant and Prodigy told Dagger the details of his husband's pyre. The child was now in the hands of Dagger; He bid Dagger a good night and then left. Dagger shut the door and stared at the only thing Inn had left behind. How could he raise a child when he didn't even know how? He had never even held a baby before. Inn knew that. How did Inn think he was qualified to look after the child?

The bundled child let out a squeak, and Dagger looked down

at the small thing. He weighed barely anything in Dagger's arms and he worried about accidentally hurting him. The birth certificate that sat on the inside table had his name listed as Wick, son of Inn, House of Prodigy. But Prodigy had clarified that he wanted that changed as soon as possible. Dagger felt a little off by Prodigy's behavior towards his son's child. His son was dead. This was his only grandson. Dagger understood that what Inn had done was dirty, not only for him, but for his parents, but that should have been settled. Inn had paid with his life for this.

Rocking the small child in his arms, Dagger called his father Risk. He needed help with the baby and the only person he could even think to call was his own father, who had parental experience. Dagger thought if anyone could help him right now and understand his pain, it would be his father. Dagger paced around with the newborn in his arms. If he held still, the infant would scream. Having this infant gave Dagger no time to mourn the loss of Inn.

When Risk showed up, the child in Dagger's arms took Risk by surprise. He hadn't expected this, Dagger hadn't even told him the details of why he had called, but had told him to come. It was an emergency. There was no time to waste.

"This is the emergency, then?"

"Yes. I need your help."

"Who's child is this?"

"Inn's."

"When did—- Oh, I understand."

"He passed away in childbirth. He left his child to me. His

father had made it clear he would like the child removed from the House Of Prodigy. As for the infant's father, he is unknown."

"He is to be your ward, then?"

"It would seem so."

"Pass me the child. Mourn the loss of your husband and your friend."

Dagger's father seemed to be the only one who understood that Dagger and Inn were not the normal expectation of Skorwn couples. They were not together, but they were together only in name. They didn't have a relationship that would have produced children, but Inn trusted him enough to pass his only child off after his death, and that meant something more than the fact he had cheated on his partner.

Risk felt for his son. He had a child now whether or not he wanted him, Dagger would honor Inn's last wish for his son. No matter the cost. He wouldn't leave the newborn to suffer without someone to love him. Inn left him with the only thing he had that meant anything.

Dagger sat in their shared room, his fingers lingering on a black sweater that hung in Inn's closet. The scent of his shampoo still lingered in the room. How had he missed the fact that Inn was with child? How had he been that ignorant of the struggles of his husband? He had only been here just days before; He claimed he had a work trip and would be home after that. What had he planned on doing with the child when he got home?

"Why? Why hadn't you been honest with me? I could have

helped you. You didn't have to do this all alone, Inn. You could have asked for my help." Dagger whispered into the empty room. Only receiving silence back.

Pain of heartbreak and loss weighed down Dagger's heart at that moment. He really didn't know how to mourn Inn when all he could think about was the newborn downstairs and how he was supposed to do right by that kid. Dropping his hand away from the sweater, Dagger made his way back downstairs to find his father walking around with the child in his arms. He was whispering to the newborn. Dagger thought to himself that Inn knew Dagger could handle looking after his son and he would have a support system if he needed help.

Dagger couldn't wipe the touch of anger he felt inside about Prodigy casting the child aside like this was his fault, but Dagger knew this is how he had always been and probably always would be. After all, Inn complained about his father's strict code and being prim and proper as the first family. Dagger hadn't had that, he was the second family after all the expectations were lower.

Inn's son, however, would be the first family, and Dagger would have to raise him with that knowledge of the first family. He thought to curse Inn for this, but the small smile that was on his lips knowing that Inn had trusted him this much did little for his saddened heart.

01 - Chapter One -

Dagger woke up early today, as it was a special day. One Dagger could say he had been waiting for, for a very long time.

Dagger could remember all the birthdays right until today, the last before Wick's awakening. The damn kid had grown into a perfect male, and Dagger found himself happy to have the male around. Inn's death had brought out many stories of Inn cheating and sleeping around. Dagger really wasn't that surprised when the stories came out, but he did his best in the face of the judgment to keep Inn's child away from the bullshit. Wick still seemed to get caught up in some of the drama surrounding Inn, but thankfully he had brushed it off and ignored it, mostly. There had been a few rough patches, but not as many as Dagger first feared and when things got rough Dagger pulled out his secret weapon, his father Risk.

Wick had been a brilliant child the rest of the time, but they were more like brothers than father and son along the way. Dagger was thankful for that. He was also very thankful that Wick looked nothing like his birth father Inn. He might not have been able to stare the kid in his face if he had.

Whoever was, Wick's father had wavy blond hair and amethyst eyes. They had been carried over to Wick. He was stunning. Dagger was the complete opposite to Wick. His hair was charcoal black and his eyes ruby coloured. Wick promised to be a stunning male in the first family bloodline once he was through his awakening. Even Prodigy, who came around after some time, seemed to be a little pleased.

Wick was already showing signs of the Awakening. He was pretty moody and didn't care to be awake. The headaches Wick had been getting were horrible, and they made him want to die. The only thing Wick wanted to do was sleep all day until the pain disappeared and his skin didn't feel six sizes too small all over.

Dagger was dressed in his white set of robes and left his room. Wick needed to be up so that his birthday celebrations could go on. Dagger couldn't smile when he knew what was going to happen. Prodigy would show up for his grandson's birthday and, like the last time, he would make horrid comments about his grandsons' eyes or hair. Prodigy was a little pleased by Wick's size and temper most times, but his looks were a far different story. Dagger hated it, but he made no moves to stop the male from coming to visit. It was far out of his hands; he had blood ties to Wick.

Opening Wick's door, the pitch-black cold air of the room hit him almost immediately as he called into the blackness.

"Come, Wick, you need to wake and get ready. You know your grandfather will be here shortly, and I want to get this part over as fast as possible."

Groans were all Dagger got back. He felt bad for dragging him out of bed for this, but it had to be done. Slowly, Dagger watched Wick get out of the bed. He was a tall male and had some muscles even before his awakening. He would be a massive male. Dagger was a fairly large male as well. He was six foot six inches; he was a happy mix of muscle and such that he was partly lean.

Dagger left Wicks' room, closing the door behind him. There was a chance that he might leave Dagger alone. Dagger, who had got used to the much younger male, felt his chest go heavy. Dagger's animus had never even shown up, but when he had met Inn, he couldn't deny the connection. But this is where the connection had got them. Inn was dead, and he was alone raising his husband's affair child. Regardless of that, Dagger thought of Inn all the time and how happy would he be to see the way Dagger had raised his son? Dagger was pleased with how Wick had turned out, given that he had no experience in raising a damn thing and often asked his own father for help.

Dagger was sipping coffee when Wick finally came down the stairs. He felt bad for the kid, this close to his awakening and having to deal with his shitty grandfather. Dagger shook his head softly when he saw what his ward was wearing. He was in the bottom layers of his robes and that was all. The black robes he usually wore were changed. Today he wore white robes, or at least the bottoms. Wick had never worn the white robes and the fact of how loose they were on his body had told Dagger that his ward had gone into his room and through his closet. Dagger knew this was all about to piss his grandfather off. Wick was of the first family and was deemed black robes to wear. It showed his status. Wick made it clear he cared little to none about his status as the first family.

"I don't fully understand why you're wearing my white robes. I think I have a clue, but you know as much as I know that will be the thorn in your grandfather's side."

"Perhaps I just want to see the older male squirm. Or maybe I just want a change."

"Either is an answer I am fine with. You are old enough to make that choice for yourself."

Dagger set his coffee down to grab the present he had got for his ward. When he came back, his empty cup sat on the table beside his ward. Wick had finished his coffee. Dagger knew better than to leave his coffee down. Wick had done this since he was a child, and even as an adult, he hadn't changed that habit.

Dagger had also noticed a bunch of strange things about Wick that had started a week before and slowly grew to be much more noticeable, such as what his ward was doing now. He felt Wicks' eyes on him, and it made him slightly uncomfortable. Wick had never spent so much time watching Dagger as he did in this week alone.

Dagger gave Wick the present and hoped it would make his day just a little better. Dagger just wanted this day to go smoother than all the rest of his birthdays.

He watched as Wick opened the box. Inside was the white

diamond wrapped in much smaller amethyst stones set in a ring. It was common that the parent of the child would buy the child the colours of the house in a ring for their awakening.

Wick smiled as he slipped it on his middle finger on the right hand. He turned towards Dagger and smirked before he spoke.

"I always knew you liked me. I mean, you raised me, so you must."

That statement told Dagger what was on Wick's mind. Dagger understood he was feeling a loss. He was longing for an actual parent. He was longing for Inn or his unknown father.

"Of course I like you. You are still alive, aren't you brat?" Dagger said softly, Fluffing Wick's already messy hair.

"We know most of the reason I'm alive is that Risk wouldn't let you let me die." Wick taunted.

"There were a few times I thought about murdering you. Like when you beat up the neighbor's kids for stealing your toys, not just as a child, but as a young teenager."

"Don't forget about when I told my grandfather he was a cranky old relic in the middle of a holiday dinner."

"It was a public dinner! I was so pissed!"

"Risk was more than proud of me."

"Of course he was! He wasn't the one who had to deal with Prodigy after the event."

"It wasn't like I left you to deal with it alone. You just didn't like everything that I had to say!"

"You were causing problems!"

"Never. I was a great kid."

"Most of the time, yes, but you had your rotten moments."

"Fair enough."

"You have turned into a great man. Soon enough, you will be completely an adult and even the crusty relic won't have a damn say in anything."

"You're not going to get all sappy on me, will you? I don't think my poor heart will handle your feelings if you do." Wick teased.

"Oh bite off, you brat."

Wick rolled his eyes at Dagger's comment and felt uneasy with the thought of being a fully fledged adult. Wick might lose his complete shit if Dagger asked him to leave now. He doubted it would happen, but he really wasn't all that sure. Wick pushed down the urge to hug Dagger and ask him how things would be from here on out? He was uneasy to know Dagger's answer to that. Wick glanced at the clock. It was getting closer and closer to the time when his grandfather would show up and ruin everything.

02 - Chapter Two -

Wick nearly vomited when his grandfather brought a male to the party to set up with Dagger. The nerve of his grandfather was bewildering. Wick was not happy with this. Wick was livid and fighting every urge to put his grandfather in his place. This was Dagger and his home, not his grandfathers. Dagger had solely been his since he was a baby and he didn't want that to change, not even now that he was a grown male. Call him childish, but Dagger was all he knew and had. He didn't want to share him. Wick had never had to share him with anyone. Wick had yet to run into his grandfather, but when he did, Wick was going to say his piece about this. He found his grandfather later with Dagger and this other male. Wicks' temper flared pretty much right away the moment he got to his grandfather.

Dagger had picked up on his ward's temper right away. No one else seemed to notice. The drink in his hand was gone in the next second as he tipped the booze down his throat. This would not go well. Wick was making his way over here, and Dagger was getting ready for a blowout. Surely he wouldn't make a scene in front of all these people, but something told Dagger his ward was going to do just that. He hadn't raised Wick to behave like this, But as he neared his awakening, he was getting bolder with every day.

Dagger, himself, was not impressed with the fact that Prodigy had brought a male for him to his grandson's birthday. This was not the place and even if it had been such, Dagger didn't need another male. He had been happy with just him and Wick for the last twenty-two. Prodigy didn't seem to understand this. This had not been the first time he tried to set Dagger up with someone he knew. But he had never tried this at such an important time. Dagger understood Wick's displeasure at the event.

"Ah! Here comes my grandson, Dagger. You could have had him clean himself up more and what the hell is my blood doing parading around in white? Surely you didn't allow him to dress that way?"

Smiling a touch, Dagger turned to Prodigy and spoke. Prodigy would not like his words either. Prodigy didn't mind shoving his status down anyone who wasn't part of the first family's throat. Dagger had got used to it, but it made many people bewildered by his behavior.

"Your grandson is an adult now. He dresses himself these days. Perhaps he finds white suits him better. Inn preferred white as well." Dagger muttered, rubbing the fact that Prodigy's late beloved Inn had preferred his life outside the first family. The room had also gone quiet just after Dagger had spoken and many of the folks here for Wick's birthday were Dagger's family. The only blood-related family Wick had in the party was his grandfather and uncle, Inn's older brother.

When Wick got up to Dagger and his grandfather, the male that was brought for Dagger ran off, Suddenly needing a drink. It was hilarious to Dagger that this male ran off. Here was a male that wanted Dagger's attention but was scared of his ward. Last time Dagger checked, that was not how to win over someone. You weren't supposed to run off when the person you are supposedly interested in, child or ward, shows up. It was just bad manners.

"Grandfather---"

"You just tell me what the hell were you think wearing white when black is---"

"Listen here, old man, I will wear what the hell I feel like! If you don't like it, too bad. You didn't raise me, Dagger did. He's the only one I have to please. You piss me off!"

"How dare you! You came from my son and you killed him----"

Dagger should have noticed the anger rise further in his ward then and stopped him, but he didn't, and thus Wick's hand flew through the air and smashed his own grandfather in the face. Dagger could even wrap his head around what his ward had done. Prodigy moved to grab Wick, but Dagger stopped Prodigy's hand with his own. His ward had never gone this far as to hit his own family. Wick had crossed the line. But so had his grandfather. Neither were on the right side.

Dagger still couldn't believe that Wick had actually hit his grandfather. He never expected him to do such a thing. Dagger definitely didn't raise him that way at all. Dagger sighed but spoke up, nonetheless.

"I believe you need to leave our home now. You have said things in our home that have no place leaving your mouth. You have clearly upset my ward and I just won't allow that here, not on this day of all days."

Dagger saw his own father coming. He was coming to defuse the situation. It was just who his father was. Dagger's father was an enormous male with whom no one, not even Prodigy, would take a chance. Risk grabbed his son's ward around the head in a headlock. This was how Risk showed love for this male, who was basically another of his sons. He had helped raise Wick almost every day of his life and adored him. Risk was beyond annoyed with Prodigy's behavior, but he wouldn't show it. The last thing Risk was going to do was give him the satisfaction he had got under his skin.

"Twenty-two, Hmm, This I don't believe. I was just carrying you around and tucking you down for a nap. There is just no way you're an adult. I don't believe it. I don't see it."

Wick was happier around Dagger's family than his own blooded family. He had always been. It was just how Dagger's family showed him love and tender care. They didn't treat him like he was a dirty mark on their status.

Wick's grandfather saw him as a mistake from the day he took his first breath and his uncle didn't even try to have a connection with him. Whereas Dagger's brothers, his father, and the rest of the family took him in with open arms, they were the only genuine family he had allowed himself to have.

Wick's Uncle removed his father and himself from the party and apologized to Dagger. Dagger knew it wasn't Inn's brother's fault that their father was just a nasty old man. It was just how he was. He cared more about his status than the health and wellness of his family. He would never change, or at least he hadn't since Dagger knew him.

Dagger turned to his ward, who was now having much fun with the family. He loved watching Wick interact with his family; It reminded him of days passed when his brothers and he had birthdays and holidays. They still had holidays, but nothing like when they were kids. They had their own kids now, and that changed everything. Dagger couldn't take all the credit for raising his ward either, Risk had honestly done the most work. Dagger looked over Wick, he looked terribly flushed to Dagger. This close to his awakening, he had to be careful with his ward. He casually walked over and laid his hand on the male's forehead. The warmth that he felt against his hand made him worry. His ward was far too warm for this to be a normal cold and with his awakening coming, this had to be just that, his awakening.

"You're really warm. Too warm now for my liking. Off to bed, you go. This has been too much for you, you are going into your awakening."

Dagger's father Risk helped Dagger take Wick upstairs to his bedroom. Wick had protested about laying down but once he touched the cold bed he didn't argue any longer, he just sunk into the cold sheets. The poor kid was going into his awakening, and it was painful and sickening.

Dagger flicked the light off, leaving his ward in the dark of his room. Risk patted Dagger on the back.

"Don't worry, it will be over soon. Wick will get through his awakening. He is a sturdy kid."

"I worry about him. It's my job. Everyone has helped me raise him this far. I don't want to hear him in pain or see him suffer. I hated it when he was a child and I hate it now. I feel powerless to help him."

Risk pulled his own child against his chest.

"You are worrying too much, I know it's not a nice thing to see someone you care about in pain, but know it will be over soon and then nothing will ever hurt him again, he will be much stronger when he wakes up."

"How did you get through all of us without worrying yourself to death?"

"After the first one, I got used to what I was doing. Trust me when I say it only takes one child to make you understand how children work, at least skorwn children. Human children are far less to worry about, not that I would have any experience with that. I just have seen some things about them. They are far easier to damage though, so I don't know if you would call it easier or harder now that I actually think about it."

03 - Chapter Three -

Dagger could hear his ward screaming in pain around two a.m. He felt bad as he got out of the bed to help his ward. Dagger's heart ached for his ward. He could remember little of his own awakening, but he knew it was painful. Opening Wick's door, the smell of vomit hit him like a ton of bricks. This was a side effect of the change, horrifying nausea. His ward wasn't in his bed, but he could see the light on in the bathroom. Heading into the bathroom, he could hardly process that the naked male in front of him was his ward. Wick was massive now, having gone through most of his awakening. This was the last part of the awakening. His ward was at least seven feet tall now. Well, that was uncommon. It was not all that rare. More so, because of his being the first family, he was going to be larger and powerful.

"It's alright Wick, I'm here to help now."

Wicks' head turned towards Dagger, and Dagger felt small under Wick now. Despite that, he too was over normal human height standards.

"It hurts so damn bad."

Wick's voice had deepened but was weakened from the awakening. His voice did something to Dagger's manhood that he was not proud of. It wasn't completely Dagger's fault. He blamed his helping his ward to the bed and his naked body, which had taken a lot out of Dagger, who sat on the end of his bed making sure his ward wasn't in any more pain. Dagger wished that one of his own brothers had stayed to help. But he had sent them away saying he could handle it.

Dagger left Wick's room and went to the kitchen. It was morning, and he hadn't even tried to sleep at all since he had helped Wick. Wick was going to need clothing and Dagger wasn't sure where to get clothing that big other than his father, but Dagger wasn't sure if his ward would want white robes or black. Wick was all Dagger could think about right now.

Dagger laid on the couch in the lounge. He would hear if Wick needed anything from here. Tossing and turning until finally; he found a spot on the couch that was more comfortable than all the rest. He closed his eyes and listened to the sounds in the house. He could hear Wick resting and that made it easier for Dagger himself to finally rest.

When Dagger woke up, he wasn't on the couch anymore; he

was in his own bed. He knew he hadn't made it there himself. He prayed Wick hadn't been the one to carry him here. He should rest still and not be overusing all his newfound strength. Listening to the sounds in the house, he could hear his father and Wick speaking downstairs. Jolting out of the bed, he stumbled over his own feet for a few steps. Dagger finally made it down the stairs and noticed Wick was wearing a large White robe. Dagger's father no doubt had brought it over.

"You should be resting. You have only just awakened." Dagger said, still more than completely exhausted.

"He's fine, leave him be." Risk said, Sipping his coffee, slowly.

"He has just gone through his awakening. He----"

"I'm more than fine, I promise."

Dagger was glad that Wick had stepped in. He might have felt the urge to argue with his father given his lack of sleep and the stress he had been under waiting for Wick to be ok most of the night. Dagger looked at his ward. But the connection Dagger felt now between them made him sick instantly. Wick was his animus. Just how was this to be? How could it be? It had to be a mistake?

Dagger looked at his father now, unable to make words. He was beyond ok with this. This was the boy he had raised, the child his husband had birthed. What level of mind games was the universe trying to play with him right now?

"Dagger, are you ok? My son?"

Risk watched his son with questioning eyes but felt like he

might know what was going on, but he would wait for more proof or someone to tell him. But his son was far from ok right now and it was clearly being displayed on his face in real-time.

Dagger turned and left the room. He needed to; He needed space. How was this even possible? He thought. This was Inn's child. This couldn't actually be true? Dagger knew you couldn't control who your animus was, but he was the child he raised, the son of his former husband. Dagger was pacing the hallway. He hadn't really even noticed he had been doing it. His own thoughts and feelings completely distracted him at this moment.

"Stop," Wick demanded sharply, his voice echoing off the walls in the hall.

Dagger turned, and Wick was in the mouth of the hall. His mouth went dry.

"I.." Dagger couldn't find words to share with Wick. This had never happened to him. He felt like he might just die at that moment.

"I know what you know. I know what we are, Dagger." Wick whispered into the hall, but the sound still reached Dagger's ears. The words made Dagger's stomach turn. It wasn't really disgust that made it turn, but it was fear, pure terror. This was wrong, so very wrong. Dagger hadn't really felt fear many times other than when he looked at his ward the first time when he was a newborn. He was terrified of how he should act and behave right now.

"I can't be this with you Wick, you have to understand why." He muttered into the silence of the hallway.

"No, You can't just decide this for yourself!" Wick yelled, his temper popping up and making Dagger worried about what his next words might bring up.

"I can, trust me. I am the older one here." The words felt nasty coming off Dagger's tongue, but it was the truth.

Wick hit the wall in fury. This pissed Dagger off to the point he yelled for Wick to go to his room. Wick immediately challenged Dagger as any adult male would. He wasn't a child anymore, Dagger knew this, but he didn't want to believe it. Dagger wanted to get his own way here, even if his ward was an adult now. He flexed his own anger now.

"You don't just get to punch things when you cannot have your own way!" Dagger snapped.

"Oh yeah, And why the hell is that?" Wick clipped back just as snappy.

"Why, you ask? Because this is my home, I don't just punch walls when I'm angry."

"Your home! This is our home." Wick snapped again, far angrier this time, even making Dagger a little more worried about his ward's behavior than ever before.

Wick was slowly backing Dagger into the corner without Dagger even realizing what he was doing. Wick knew that this wasn't a good idea to do this. He had seen how angry his guardian could get when cornered, but he knew he could handle the anger.

When Dagger's back hit the wall, he knew his ward had bested him. They were both panting from screaming at each other. Dagger's anger was subsiding. He was ready to just walk away, but Wick opened his mouth and spoke. The air chilled around them. Dagger felt a wave of anger like he had never had before.

"You're mine. I've owned you from the day I was born. That is not about to change now."

Dagger felt his fists ball up and when Dagger punched Wick, he should have felt better, surely. But no, he really just felt disgusted with himself. Dagger never wanted to hit his ward, even worse his animus. His hand ached with the pain of hitting his beloved, someone he was supposed to love and cherish. He had never hit Wick, not even as a child, when he misbehaved.

Dagger felt so dirty. He wanted to make sure Wick was ok at that moment, but it was clear he was livid and needed his own time.

Dagger stomped off to his room. He slammed his bedroom door and had to remind himself here; he was an adult. He thought strongly about tossing his room into an oblivion of destruction, but he was all too aware his father was here and would hear him.

Laying back on his bed, Dagger clenched his hand, the one he had hit Wick with, and felt like shit again. He clenched his own hand so hard he feared he might break his own hand.

He was more than annoyed with himself. He should have had restraint and explained to Wick why things couldn't be this way, but no, he hit him.

Dagger was still beating himself up an hour later, but now he had settled into the thought that it wasn't all his fault and while he regretted hitting Wick. He would not apologize first, it just wouldn't happen.

04 - Chapter Four -

Dagger sat by himself in his room still, not yet having left. His father had not been a witness to what Dagger had done. He didn't see it, but he had positively heard it. From the smashing of things downstairs, Dagger knew Wick was still pretty angry. Dagger wanted to scream, yell and trash his room, but that wouldn't get him far. He was two centuries too old to act like that. Wick was not. He was also having an influx of all kinds of hormones, and that would not help with this. With not so much as another thought, Dagger's stomach growled, and he sighed. Dagger needed food, but he didn't want to even face his father. He felt guilty. By now, Dagger's father had to know something. Wick wasn't exactly being quiet about his anger. Dagger wasn't sure what to tell his father if he dared ask what the cause of all this was. He couldn't lie to his father, but the truth left a sour taste in his mouth.

Dagger left his room and went downstairs. He needed food pretty badly. Wick and his father were at the table now, Wick having seemed to have calmed down and they both made no move to notice Dagger. Dagger smiled to himself. His father had done this to Dagger when he was a child. When they had fought, he would ignore Dagger until Dagger had calmed down and reigned in his anger. Risk did this so that Dagger and his brothers would self reflect on their behavior and understand their emotions better. Dagger had never taken that approach to raise his ward. Wick had never got angry with him regularly until recently, but he had just weighed that up to be the awakening. He was a great kid and would be a better man than Dagger could ever be; he knew that for sure. Grabbing a much-needed cup of coffee, Dagger sat down at the table and sipped it slowly. Call him immature for a two hundred and thirty-four-year-old man, but he was not about to say sorry first. He was positive about that. Dagger was being petty. There was no lie about that, but he really didn't care now. He could be petty.

Risk looked at both the boys. Wick was not even acknowledging Dagger's presence and Dagger. You could see he was not ready to say sorry. These boys were his sons. One knew it down to his blood well, the other did not. Risk sighed, but not outwardly. They were both being dramatic, Dagger a little more dramatic than Wick, but Dagger had been that way from the time he was little. Risk could sense something between the boys from day one. No male worth his salt would accept a child born outside the wedding. Even if that child belonged to his deceased husband, it just didn't happen. Risk would bet on his firstborn son's life that these two were animus's. Risk felt for his son deeply. Inn's death had wreaked his son. For the first three months of Wick's life, Dagger was quiet and unsure of how to process his situation. Risk had been there whenever Dagger had called and even stayed for a few weeks to help.

Risk and Prodigy had set them up because Dagger was on top of everything, his classes, his training, his magic, and he wasn't even the first family. Dagger was well on track for many achievements, but he gave that all up to give Inn everything he wanted. He had taken leave from his career to travel and explore with Inn after they were married. He allowed Inn to spend his money without a care in the world; It was how Dagger had the house where he lived. They had bought it together as an important step in their future. Risk had even thought at one point he might have had a grandchild, but then everyone was blindsided with Wick.

Many details about Wick were still unknown to everyone, but that didn't stop Dagger from loving the kid. After all, Inn had become a close friend to Dagger, someone he might have been able to love if the time had been right.

Risk had to address what was going on here before it caused a rift.

"Alright, brats, tell me how long you intend to ignore what we all know, And don't lie to me. I know you both all too well for that to be passable?"

Dagger paled as he looked at his father. How did he know? The smile on Wicks' face told him all the things he couldn't.

Risk sipped his coffee slowly, thinking over his words before he spoke.

"Would I be correct to assume that you are each other's animus?"

"Yes,"

"No, not at all."

Wick sighed before standing up and attempting to walk away from the table. Risk grabbed his arm and pulled him back to the table. Wick was annoyed with Dagger's behavior and he was struggling with wanting to do something about it. But his caretaker had already hit him for pushing him to his limit, Which Wick was all too aware of. He had seen Dagger lose his temper. Dagger still to this day remained unaware that he had spied on him.

"All right boys, it's time to get along. Whether or not you'd like it, you guys are basically soulmates, beloved partners, and so on. There's no way you guys are going to escape it, so you better just get cushy with the idea. Now."

"I'm more than fine with the idea but your son Dagger, however, is not something about how he raised me or whatever. It's not like we are actually related!"

"Real mature Wick, because that's how you win me over." Dagger snapped sarcastically, not wanting to even touch on how badly those words had hurt him. He shoved the feeling down. He could deal with that another time.

Risk watched as Dagger and Wick continued to fight. The anger in the room rose to a level that made Risk decide they needed to work this out on their own. Without either of the boys looking away from their argument, Risk slipped away. His boys had issues only they could work out. Risk could understand why his son was not okay with Wick being his beloved partner. He had raised the boy from a newborn. But, at the same time, Risk worried that would put his son off true happiness. Risk knew he might have to force the relationship between them at first, but if that's what he had to do, then so be it. He would.

Dagger glared at the spot where Risk had been sitting only a few minutes before. Of course, his father had made the slip, Dagger would make the slip too if he could. His house or not. Looking at the clock, it was only three in the afternoon and he still hadn't grabbed lunch. That was the whole reason he had even come down. He was hungry.

Wick must have been thinking the same thing. He got up and opened the door to the fridge. Dagger watched him pick out all the ingredients to make a turkey bacon club sandwich. It must have also been a peace offering because it was Dagger's favorite kind of sandwich.

Wick knew where to place his bets when it came to making Dagger forgive him. Dagger was a sucker for food, though you could never tell because Skorwn had a lightning-fast metabolism. They hardly ever gained weight after their awakening. It was just unheard of.

Wick pushed the plate towards Dagger. Dagger took the plate more roughly than he had intended. He ate the sandwich slowly and enjoyed every bite. Dagger was famished and still pretty tired. He was also kicking himself in the butt for not taking the time he had spent pouting and using it for a nap. He would have benefited from that better than just sitting on his bed in anger.

Wick made himself two sandwiches of his own and sat one seat over from Dagger. He was worried Dagger might move, but he didn't, which gave Wick a feeling of calm. They ate in silence but it was a comfortable silence, Not an angry silence like it had been. Perhaps they might be able to make this work. If Dagger could get over the weirdness of Wick being his husband's child, who he had to spend many years raising?

Dagger thought about why he had been ok with raising the child. It wasn't his, and they weren't family, but he had provided and sheltered the kid every single day of his life. Hell, he had even saved the kid from Prodigy every single time he could, and that alone was a larger task than you would think.

Looking at Wick, Dagger couldn't deny the feeling of them being beloved partners, but he feared ruining everything he had built for this kid. It wasn't just his feelings he had to consider here, his ward's feelings were also front and center. It was all so much more intense for him as well; he hadn't even had a chance to be comfortable in his newly awakened powers. Before it slammed him with urges much more demanding than either wanted to acknowledge.

05 - Chapter Five -

Dagger woke up with a fresh start to the day. He tried not to notice how his ward had taken up a spot in his much larger than a king-sized bed. He had promised to try to make this work for his ward, So Wick in his bed was something he would not whine about at least right now. His ward woke up shortly after he finished making their breakfast. He almost choked on his coffee when his ward came into view. The five o'clock shadow he was sporting was deadly against his handsome face. He hadn't expected it, not one bit.

"I need—I need to—-Um. Wow, I need to do something." Dagger mumbled out as he left the room. His brain was confused, and he was feeling annoyed, but also it horrified

Dagger that in the face of his ward he couldn't even form a fucking sentence. That had never happened to him, ever. He punched the door in frustration and as if to be the thorn in his side, he heard his ward yell about how when they got mad they weren't allowed to punch shit, or so Dagger had said just days before.

"It's my house, I'll punch it if I want." Dagger hissed out, not actually loud enough that Wick would hear him.

Wick was getting on his nerves. Going to get dressed, he dragged on his clothing. Out of the corner of his eye, he noticed the black robe. It was the only one he had kept. It had been the one he married Inn in. His heart clenched at the thought. He really wasn't sure why, even now, he still had it. He should have got rid of it, but he didn't. Whether that was because it had cost a pretty large amount of money or it was the sentimental value of it, it remained.

Wick watched from the doorway. Despite even calling his name, it was clear that he didn't notice him. He watched as Dagger made a face. That black robe he noticed tucked back in the very back of the closet must have meant something to him. Wick thought it must have had something to do with his father, Inn. He really wasn't sure why Dagger kept that stuff, all the photos and the belongings of them. It was like he wanted Wick to be jealous of it. Wick left the room. Jealousy filled his gut like the worst of pains, just like he knew it would. He was jealous of his own dead father. It wasn't the first time Wick had been jealous of his dead father, either.

He couldn't understand why, even after twenty-years Dagger was still so devoted to Inn. His father was nothing but bones by this point. He cheated on Dagger and even dropped a baby that was not his on him, and Dagger still felt something for him. Wick was pretty sure of that. He wasn't so bothered with all the photos, only the wedding photo of them. It struck Wick in a tender spot he hated to admit he had. It made him livid. Dagger had done so much for his father, only to have it all wasted.

"Wick, Come on, We need to go to the market to get you something to wear every day. You have definitely grown and will not fit into anything I own and I highly doubt my father will want to have to replace his entire wardrobe when you steal all his clothing, besides you also need some black robes, you have none."

"I need robes, yes, but I'll pass on the black ones."

"Unfortunately, that you can't. You need black robes. You don't have to wear them if you don't want to, but you need them."

"I won't wear them. It will be a waste."

"Then let them be a waste, end of the story."

Dagger sensed the air around Wick was charged with violent energy. That mainly happened when you were experiencing rage, anger, jealousy or, likewise, feelings. He wanted to ask about the male's feelings, but he also didn't want to piss him off. Dagger had never been so annoyed with himself before. Had this happened before he found out they were beloved partners, he would have just busted down all of Wick's personal walls and asked him what the hell was going on. Now it felt like he couldn't do that. That pissed him off.

Heading out, they walked for a while until they came to the only place Dagger had ever got clothing for them. Yes, it cost a pretty penny, but it was worth it to have custom robes made.

"Wick, I expect you to be on your best behavior and act your age. It's very important you don't make a scene here. Or you will not have nice clothing."

"It's not the first time you have brought me into public. Relax."

Dagger fought the urge to bite back a nasty comment. Instead, he took Wick's arm lightly and pulled him inside to get sized up for both colors of the robes. The women that were sizing up Wick told Dagger it would be an hour before Wick was free from the sizing process. Dagger left Wick to finish the rest of the running around the market he had to do.

Wick just stood around and put up with the lady touching him. As much as he hated to feel her touch him, he didn't voice that or even make any move that would have said that. The last thing he wanted was to upset Dagger.

The seamstress's hands were gentle on his skin, and she made light conversation with him.

"You are of the first family, yes?"

"Yes, unfortunately."

"Can't say that's the first time I've heard that."

"Is it common then?"

"Not really, but I've heard it."

"Really, I didn't expect that."

"There are a lot of things you don't expect to hear when you work here."

"Fair enough."

She fitted the black robe on him, checking for any size changes. She didn't seem pleased with the robe on him.

"Something wrong?"

"You just don't look like the type for black robes, but Dagger has had me make one for the last twenty years, I'm assuming for you?"

"Yes, I don't wear them if I'm honest."

"Nothing wrong with that. Dagger wasn't a fan of them when Inn was alive. They forced him to wear them at social gatherings, but outside of that, everything he wore was white. His husband was the same way, despite being born of the first family."

"I prefer the white as well."

Wick was aware that those around him knew of where he came from, but not how he came to be. Prodigy was quick to bury his whole birth story. Many knew he was Inn's son, but always seemed to be taken aback when they finally saw his looks. He didn't look like his guardian; he looked like his unknown father. Whoever he actually was.

"I'm not surprised. You were raised by Dagger and his

father, Risk. Not your grandfather, Prodigy. Thank the heavens there. Dagger makes a good stand-in father."

Wick could only think about how he could blow this lady's mind if he told her the entire truth, that Dagger wasn't his stand-in father, but his beloved partner and Risk is the closest thing he had to a father. Dagger had never tried to play Wick's father. Wick knew why, too. Dagger wasn't his father and didn't think that title was fitting for him. But Dagger got upset when Wick reminded him they weren't actually related. Wick had seen it.

When she slipped the white robe on him, she stepped back and inspected him.

"Yes, White is definitely more your color. Matches your eyes nicely."

"Thank you."

She hammered him with many more questions as she adjusted things on his robes and he thought he might go deaf before she stopped talking. He felt terrible to think that, but she was actively giving him a headache and he wanted to tell her to shut up, but she had been nice to him thus far. She had also only accidentally stabbed him with the sewing needle once.

"Would you like anything to drink quickly?"

"Could I have a glass or bottle of water, please?"

She left the room, and he looked at the clock. Dagger was getting dangerously close to being late to come back and get him. Wick sighed. This sucked. He would much rather waste this time with Dagger.

When she finally returned, she gave him his water and finished the last touches of his last white robe. Now having finished with Wick, they let him sit down finally. He glanced at the clock again and noticed Dagger had been gone for over an hour. Dagger had told him an hour top, So where in the half acres of hell was his beloved partner?

He was getting pretty annoyed and was worried if this lady kept asking him any more questions. He might ask her to shut up and that would look bad for Dagger.

06 - Chapter Six-

Dagger was really late. His watch told him it had been an hour and a half since he left Wick at the clothing shop. He prayed Wick had been a gentleman to the ladies in the shop and not a right jerk. He had been going there for such a long time and never once had poor service. If Wick ruined that, he was going to kick his butt. As soon as he walked into the store, he noticed Wick was sipping a coffee, talking with two reception ladies.

He saw Wick notice him. Before Dagger could even get the words 'I'm sorry I'm late' out of his mouth, Wick had spoken, and the words made Dagger jumpy.

"You're late, *Sweetheart.*"

Just by the way his ward had spoken the word sweetheart, he knew Wick was mad. Oh well, he was the parent metaphorically in this deal, not Wick. So he could suck it up.

"Lose the attitude Wick, I had to get the other things, such as the food you need when you run a household. I had a lot to do."

"Mhmm."

"Time to go. We have more things to do."

Dagger would pay the last bill for the clothing when it got dropped off at their home in a few days, three at the very most. Wick was in a mood now, and it did not impress Dagger either, but he was happy that Wick had maintained his good spirits around the ladies.

Wick said little as they headed out for lunch. Heading to a restaurant they went to often, Dagger didn't even have to ask Wick what he wanted to eat since he only ever ordered the same thing. Which was a good thing, since Wick had chosen not to speak to Dagger right now. Dagger honestly felt bad for the kid, he was being bombarded with so much only days into his change and he didn't want to tell his ward that they had been invited to come for a public dinner in a few days and that was why he actually needed the black set of robes. Dagger didn't want to argue with Prodigy in public if Wick showed up in white.

They ate in silence and Dagger felt like he should tell Wick to grow up and act his age, but he refrained because that would probably only make things worse. Wick finished his food before Dagger, but that was because Dagger was only picking at his food absentmindedly.

"Eat your food, Dagger, don't just pick at it."

Dagger looked up at his ward, who was frowning at him pretty intensely. The urge to tell him off was there, but he just took larger bits of his food to stop him from responding to his ward's comment. It wasn't worth him making a scene in public.

Once Dagger finished his food, he went up and paid for their meals. Wick stacked all the plates and utensils to make it easier for the server to clean the table. Wick waited for Dagger to come back to the table and grab his coat before he stood up and followed Dagger out of the restaurant.

Dagger took them to a small cafe so he could grab a coffee and Wick could get a hot chocolate, because he didn't drink coffee after twelve in the afternoon. While they were waiting in line. Wick tried to pass Dagger money for their order, but Dagger wouldn't accept it. He instead ignored Wick, so much so that Wick sighed loudly.

"Did you need something?"

"You ignored my attempts to pay for our drinks,"

"What does it matter? It's my money on both cards, regardless."

A sick feeling settled in Wick's stomach at that remark, even though it was true. He felt pretty terrible that he was using Dagger's money; he had never even thought about it until now.

"Please find out how much of your money I've spent, and I'll attempt to repay it. I'm sure I could grab up a job somewhere."

Dagger should have known Wick would take his words out of context and be bothered by them. It made Dagger feel pretty shitty, but now in the cafe waiting for their drinks was not the place to discuss this. With their drinks in hand, they walked home in silence; They were walking down the sidewalk almost at their gate when Wick spoke again.

"You're acting like an angry stay-at-home parent. What have I done now?"

Dagger choked on the coffee they had picked up at the small cafe place only about ten minutes before. Whipping around to face Wick, he took a deep breath before he spoke, rudely. He had finally had enough of all his behavior today.

"Perhaps if you stopped acting like a spoiled brat and reigned in your newfound attitude, I wouldn't have to act like an angry stay-at-home parent, or better yet, I wouldn't have to act like your mother."

"Well then, *Mother*, I finally understand where your anger must come from. Your heat must be a terrible thing."

Dagger had no other nasty words to present to his ward, so instead, he walked away or stomped away if you could do that down a sidewalk. Getting in the house first, Dagger wanted to lock him outside, but again, that was not something a mature two-hundred-year-old did.

Wick finally had enough with Dagger now, too. It clouded his mind with jealousy and anger. Standing inside the living room, he looked at the walls. There were photos of his father Inn on the walls. The wedding photo was the one he went after. He hated that thing the most. He ripped the damn thing off the wall and threw it at the tiled floor; The smash was the greatest sound he ever heard. He felt like it finally felt like this house was his home. Their home. Not just a home where he lived along with Dagger and his father's everything shoved so far down his throat, it was hard to ignore it.

The next photo he grabbed was some kind of party and Dagger looked stunning, but the male next to him, not so much. He froze, looking down the hall towards the kitchen. His eyes locked with Daggers. He wasn't aiming at eradicating this one, because it didn't bother him as much as the wedding photo did, but he was furious, so he didn't care. He would ruin them all.

"You put that back. Now! Those are very important to me!"

Dagger was visibly shaking from head to toe. Wick actually felt worried for a moment that Dagger might smite him for this. He was worried about Dagger and felt something in him that might have been guilt, but he pushed it away. His hatred was front and center.

"This shit needs to go now, more so that one! I fucking hate it. I hate him! I hate it all."

"You don't get to decide that! This is my home and I'll hang what I want to on the walls, and that man brought you into this world. Don't you dare speak those words when you talk about him!"

The frame in Wicks' hand sailed at the floor as he wiped it towards there. Dagger's eyes went black. Wick knew then he was in shit again. His guardian was so furious. The pictures fell as the walls shook as Dagger stalked towards Wick. Dagger's hand came up, and he thought he might actually hit Wick again, but he didn't. Instead, he just yelled in irritation. He was beyond livid with his ward right now.

"How dare you act like such a freaking brat! This is my house and you have no right to ruin my things because you're jealous or whatever! That man was my best friend. He was here well before you!"

"How dare I? How dare you! We are animus, beloved partners, soul mates. Have you thought about how I might feel that you still love my long since dead father and choose him over me?"

"I have not chosen him over you! How do you figure that one? Those photos have been there longer than you have been alive!"

"I want them gone! The wedding photo the most!"

"You don't get what you want!"

All Dagger heard of the whole thing Wick had yelled at him was how he loved Wick's father. He had once, but not in a long time. His throat was sore from all the screaming they were doing and had been doing lately, as he turned and walked to pick up the glass and broken frames.

Forcing down the urge to slap the brat around some more and scream till he couldn't, he just took a few deep breaths before he spoke sternly, Making sure the kid would finally understand something.

"Just so we are clear, Wick, I didn't love your father. It was out of duty. We were best friends. Nothing more. He proved that when he gave birth to you."

07 - Chapter Seven-

It had been a week since Dagger and Wick had spoken for more than a minute at a time. Neither of them wanted to be in the same room for significantly long after the picture incident. Dagger, however, had taken down all the photos of Inn. Dagger was ashamed to admit he was fearful that Wick would ruin the rest of the photos of his best friend if he left them up. Wick had made it very clear to Dagger that the photos were not welcome in the home, even if the person, his father, was long dead. Wick just couldn't get a handle on his jealous behavior when he saw the damn photos.

Dagger couldn't help but feel bad that Wick thought Dagger loved his father. Wick was out of the loop when it came to

Dagger's once relationship with Inn. They were married just so Dagger made Inn look good and this had worked for a while. Dagger was a straight arrow, never cheated, never got into any kind of trouble with the imperial police. Inn was forever in trouble. He had been arrested, but his father had shoved the charges under the mat so we would never see them. Prodigy and Risk put together the marriage. All parties got royalties out of the marriage. For Dagger, he got a status boost and a husband, also a hefty amount of money, that he too this day hadn't touched. He was sure at some point he would give it to Wick. It was no use to him; it felt like dirty money now.

When Dagger had slid the box of photos into the closet to put into proper storage later. His fingers brushed a familiar feeling envelope. It was the one that had been written just days before Inn had died according to the mail date. The letter had arrived a week after Wick had been given to Dagger. The letter told Dagger that Inn was sorry he died, but he was not sorry about the way he died. It also explained why Dagger had got Wick. The letter simply said the reason Dagger had got Wick was because that was what the fates wanted. They had told him so before he died. They didn't want Dagger to be lonely since Inn was going to pass away. Dagger had just assumed it was fear that made Inn write that. Perhaps he had been scared Dagger would abandon the newborn, but Dagger hadn't. Dagger could abandon the newborn, it just wasn't in him.

Wick sat at the kitchen table, his coffee in his hands. He was pretty ready to admit he was wrong about the photos, but Dagger had taken them down, agreeing that they didn't belong on the walls anymore. That made Wick sick deep in his stomach. He felt wrong to be mad at his own father, who passed long ago. It pained Wick that Dagger and he hadn't talked in days. He wanted to block Dagger in a room and force him to talk to him. He didn't care if it was negative attention his animus gave him, he just wanted his lover to give him attention. He was hungry for Dagger's attention.

Wick watched Dagger come into the kitchen. His sweater had dust caked on the back. That must have meant Dagger had gone into the attic. That was the only place Wick knew to be crazy dusty. Dagger had forbidden Wick from going into the attic because there were things of sentimental value up there, and Wick was sure it was more of Inn's stuff. Wick sipped his coffee slowly, finally deciding he would apologize to his lover. But he wasn't sure what word he should use. What he had done wasn't just a minor accident. He had destroyed things that meant a lot to Dagger, Even if Wick couldn't understand why.

"I'm really sorry about what happened. I shouldn't have thrown your photos. They mean something to you. Even If they piss me off beyond anything else."

Dagger went on like he hadn't heard Wick, and that angered him. Dagger had heard him though, he just wasn't ready to talk about what had happened. He would not let it show that Dagger ignoring him had upset him, though; he had to prove not just to Dagger but himself, that when he didn't get his own way, he would not throw a fit. Now, he was an adult. After all, it was time he acted like it. Even if that meant pushing aside his unwarranted jealousy for his dead father and all their memories.

Thinking for a moment, Wick drank back the rest of his coffee before he stalked towards the kitchen sink where Dagger was washing dishes. Getting in Dagger's space was not a good idea right now, and he was aware of that. But, He stood right behind Dagger, getting close until he pressed himself against the older male's back, enjoying the feeling of being able to touch Dagger even if only for a moment. He set his coffee cup in thc sink. Dagger had stopped washing dishes and just stood completely still. Dagger was unsure what to do at that moment. Wick took this chance, now having Dagger's attention to lean down and whisper in the older male's ear.

"I'm sorry Dagger. I'm sorry I made you take down the photos. It wasn't fair to you. I just—- I'm sorry again."

Leaving the kitchen, Wick sighed. This was going to be so hard for him to just ignore the gnawing feeling inside that made him angry about the way Inn, His own father, had treated Dagger and Dagger was still ok with that. Even now.

Both Dagger and Risk had taught Wick meditation, but he hardly took the time to do it. It was something a lot of Skorwn used to hone and train their powers, but it was also used to help relax and calm one's soul. Right now, Wick felt like his soul could use a lot of calm. That thing was probably like the lawless wild west right now.

Taking a deep breath, He headed to the mediation room. The scent of incense hit him like a brick and made him sigh deeply. It had been a long time since he had been in this room, and way before he had awoken. With all the power that the Skorwn possessed, it took a lot to calm it.

Making sure he wasn't tracking any dirt or mess into the room, he wiped his feet off on the mat and went inside. The fire that was always lit, using Dagger's powers, of course, welcomed him into the space. It danced around the glass shell containing it. Wick smiled softly, getting down to sit on the floor.

When was the last time his guardian was in the room? He wondered. He crossed his legs and set his palms flat on his knees. After taking deep breaths of the incense in the room, he was calm. The Skorwn didn't believe in a god, because they themselves were like gods, but they believed in fate.

Wick was sure fate was angry with him. With everything he had been doing, he really wouldn't be surprised if fate was. This time, meditating would be significant. He had yet to do so since his awakening. Dagger and Risk had taught Wick everything about what came after your awakening, the powers, A sword that lived in the void, made of your own blood cast into metal, The houses in which you lived, and the custom to give gifts for the awakening. Normally it was something to signify your house colors, but Wick had clarified that was something he would not want. Thus, he did not have a piece of jewelry with his house color or colors on it.

He closed his eyes and really focused on his meditation now. He knew Dagger would be aware he was in meditation, he could feel it. After all, it linked the room to Dagger by his fire. That realization didn't bother him in the slightest.

Taking a deep breath, the incense further calmed him and he slipped into a state of relaxation, one he hadn't felt before. It was like sleeping, but being fully aware of every feeling in your body. If he had any wounds, they would have been healed now, thanks to the meditation. He could feel his powers swirling inside of him, flowing through every part of his core, right down to his soul. The warmth of his powers was a gentle heat that seemed like a warm hug as it moved through him. He was comfortable with it. That was a good thing.

He thought of all the lessons from Risk, when he told him about a calming total relaxation, one that heals the soul and mind. Wick was sure he had found that total relaxation.

08 - Chapter Eight -

Wick was doing what he promised himself. He was going to grow up a little more for Dagger; he deserved it. He only knew one male he could confide in about trying to grow up more and be what Dagger needed. Risk. Dagger's father helping him was about the only way Wick thought he could mature more and be the man that Dagger needed and Dagger would want. Sitting at Risk's dining table, he finally got the courage to ask the male for help. This man was the most like his own father, after all.

"Risk, I need help, I really do."

"Do you, or do you need more time to adjust to your new well, everything?"

"I need help to grow into a male Dagger would be happy to be around and proud of. I make him so angry with me sometimes and I can't stop it. I'm so terribly jealous of what he had with my father. It's wrong of me too."

"Dagger is already proud of you, no matter what you do, Wick."

"But He isn't. I did something I'm honestly not proud of, and I feel terribly guilty about it."

Wick went on and explained what he had done. The picture incident and pissing Dagger off. Wick could see Risk was thinking deeply after now, knowing what Wick had done. Wick knew what he had done was cross a line that shouldn't have been. But there was nothing he could do now other than attempt to fix it. Looking down into his hands, Wick waited for Risk to say something. He knew it disappointed Risk as well, he could feel it, but Risk made no move to act on his disappointment.

"I can understand where Dagger would be upset about all this, but he also needs to have some understanding for you as well. But that doesn't excuse what you did. You know your father is a sore spot for Dagger. He wishes he could have done more for him."

"I know. I know this all too well."

"Then you know you need to understand that there will always be parts of Inn in that house that you can't get rid of. You need to accept that. I know that is no straightforward task."

"I told Dagger I hated my father. I said it in the heat of the moment, but I meant it and he knew it."

"Oh, Wick, you don't hate him."

"But I do. I hate the way he treated Dagger and the way Dagger still protects his image and his everything."

"You don't hate him, you hate things about him."

"I hate a lot of things about him, though."

"Dagger will most likely feel he failed to raise you properly because of this, he is probably struggling with his own issues right now too."

"But he raised me properly, I just can't stand Inn. I can't. Everything about him makes me angry."

"While that may be true. He is still your father and you know that."

"It doesn't mean I have to like him or what he has done."

"You're right, you don't have to like him and what he has done. That alone proves you were raised right, but for Dagger, it's the fact that you hate Inn."

"I know."

"Dagger is complicated. You need to approach this all differently."

Wick and Risk chatted about Dagger and the best way to help him. They came up with many ideas and ways to make it easier for him. It was just a matter of seeing how they worked on Dagger.

Dagger sat at home, his coffee in one hand and the Tv remote in the other hand. He felt lonely.

Even with Wick in the house, when he was home, of course, he was still lonely. Dagger saw less and less of him every day. This hammered the fact home that if he pushed Wick away, he really would be all alone. It worried him.

Flicking off the Tv, He went to do something. Dagger reached out to his father Risk, only to be told he was pretty busy with a project and couldn't hang out with him. Wick was with him and they were doing things together. Dagger thought about hanging out with his brothers or perhaps some cousins, but no one really seemed to stand out. Dagger would much rather have hung out with Risk and Wick, but it seemed that was the club he wasn't allowed to join right now.

Dagger decided he would venture into the basement and grab a vintage, something to lighten his mood. In the basement, Dagger had a crate of wine. They aged it for a decent length of time; It had been a gift from a human he saved many years before when he was just an adult himself. Dagger was pretty sure that was the last time he was outside of the walls of the Skorwn's closed off void. Maybe he would have to take a trip, interact with humans again. It might do him a little good to see humans again.

The basement was dark and pretty cold. But it was clean. Once only a few years ago it had been used as Wick's toy room, but Wick grew up and the toy room just became another space in the basement. It had been a massive toy room, Dagger and Risk, along with everyone else, had spared no expense to make sure Wick wanted for nothing. Dagger still made sure Wick wanted for nothing. Now that Wick was an adult, Dagger thought about talking to Pyro, the leader of the entire city of Skorwn, and asked to be cleared to head back to work. He had worked for Pyro a few times before he went off to give Inn and then Wick everything they needed.

Pyro had offered him a job on his personal team, a hired soldier, and he had been so close to expecting it. But Inn wanted him to take time off work for them.

Wick sat at the table, wondering what Dagger was doing. The male was forever on Wick's mind.

"I think the first part of you growing up is learning about the houses you are born from and live in."

Wick thought about that for a moment. He had done a bit in school to learn about his houses, mainly Dagger's, but also Risk and Dagger had taught him what the school couldn't. But, He really knew nothing about Inn's house. The house of Prodigy. It confused him as to why Inn didn't belong to the house of Dagger. They had lived in their own home and were married.

"Hey, Risk, question?"

"Yes, Son?"

"Why didn't Inn belong to the house of Dagger?"

"Oh, He didn't belong to the house of Dagger because he didn't want to lose his status as the first family."

"That's wrong."

"It was his choice."

"He chose wrong. Honestly, I would rather belong to the house of Dagger vs the house of Prodigy."

"Inn had a different view on that, but it was his first family title that kept him out of a lot of trouble. Inn loved to cause problems. It was one reason he asked Dagger to take leave from his job."

"Yes, Dagger has shown me a few photos from when he was working and some of his achievements. He is brilliant."

"Yes, He is. I think he would benefit from heading back to work now that he can."

"I feel bad that he didn't head back after Inn, But then he was handed me and I'm sure that broke his heart even more. He couldn't go back to work, something he loved."

"Yes, He loved his job, but he made you a promise when he saw you. He would look after you and take care of you. You were the most important thing to him then and I'm sure if you asked him, he would still say that now. I'm almost positive about that."

"I sure hope so. Sometimes, he is all I can bear to think about. It's overwhelming, but I have been good at managing it."

"Don't let it get to be too much before you be honest with Dagger and tell him how much he is on your mind."

Dagger had hunted down one of the best wines in the basement and brought it upstairs. He poured himself a glass before relaxing on the sofa again. This time, though, he had the photo album. It was full of photos of Wick growing up over the years. Wick had never once seen any of the photos, mostly because Dagger hoarded them to himself. They were his favorite; they made him think of all the significant memories they had together and all the fun things they had done. But also, they just reminded Dagger it was all real, and he had raised Wick to adulthood, safely.

Dagger had really never noticed how much the brat had grown since he turned eighteen.

Hunger nipped at Dagger and he danced his drunk behind all the way to the kitchen, where he made a feeble attempt at making a clean dinner. All while, still drinking way more than he needed, and he drank way more than he thought he had. He should have known he was pushing his boundaries when it came to his tolerance for alcohol, but he didn't.

09 - Chapter Nine -

Dagger was still completely drunk, less than he had been earlier, but still drunk when Wick finally came home. He barely even understood that Wick was home. He was more so looking around the room at the mess. Dagger had cooked or tried to cook spaghetti and meatballs. The red sauce was everywhere, Including the burner on the stovetop. It looked as if a red sauce bomb had gone off in the entire kitchen. That being said, Dagger was by far the dirtiest thing in the kitchen. It covered him from head to toe in sauce, and he looked more confused than Wick was.

Wick could hardly understand how his animus and guardian had messed up the complete kitchen like that. Looking around the kitchen, he spotted the empty bottle of wine and put the total story together in his head. Dagger got drunk, got hungry, and destroyed the kitchen. Wick was beyond surprised that Dagger had drank alcohol, Dagger rarely drank, ever.

Wick knew he was in no position to yell at Dagger about this, but come the morning he was going to rip his lover a new one. What Dagger had done was completely dangerous. He could have killed himself at worst and at best burned down the entire house. His lover was now passed out at the table still covered in red sauce and Wick smiled, seeing how peaceful he looked in the moment. Wick carefully picked him up and took him to his bedroom. Instead of sliding his marinated lover in the bed, He took him to the shower.

Dagger woke up when Wick undressed him. Wick had moved him around too much and alerted his drunken senses.

Dagger opened his eyes and looked up at Wick. It confused him how he had got this way. Wick finally got Dagger undressed. He didn't bother to look at the naked body of his lover because he knew there would be another time for that. Right now, he needed to make sure his lover was clean before tucking him into his bed. The lack of a bathtub in Dagger's bathroom annoyed Wick. He couldn't imagine how hard it had been when he was a small child to bathe him without the tub. He had one of two choices: get naked and shower with Dagger to save his clothing or shower with Dagger and his clothing, and just call it all a loss. He chose to shower with his clothing on and if Dagger sobered up a bit more than he was, it wouldn't look bad. It would be an act of care and not one of the dirty things. He also wouldn't feel like a pervert for helping him then.

Turning on the shower, Wick tested the water on his hand

before he helped his lover off the toilet where he had been positioned. Wick was careful, so very careful, to get his lover into the shower without accidentally hurting him.

Supporting Dagger's weight was pretty easy for Wick, Not because Dagger was tiny and a smaller sized male but because Wick was super built. He had easily put on a hundred pounds of muscle since his awakening and grew over an entire foot.

The shower definitely helped sober up Dagger, more so Dagger's manhood, which had been stirring awkwardly. Dagger knew faintly that Wick was in the shower with him. The wet clothing against his back told him Wick was still fully clothed. Dagger hadn't meant to moan when Wicks' hand rubbed the cloth over his shoulders, but he did. It was like a massage in the best of places. Dagger briefly felt Wick pull away and then go back to scrubbing him. He wasn't really even looking at Dagger; he was more worried about getting this done and over with.

Dagger was pretty drunk after the shower had done some sobering him up a fair bit. Dagger took Wick's help when he offered his help to get out of the shower and to dry off.

Wick grabbed a towel out of the linen cupboard and shook it out, fluffy and warm in his hands. Dagger would probably appreciate it. He had set Dagger back on the toilet and knelt down with the towel to dry Dagger's feet and legs off. After taking Dagger's left foot, he dried him off. He moved up his leg, making sure that Dagger was sufficiently dry before moving on to the other leg and doing the same.

Wick was well aware of how Dagger was when he got out of the shower. He rarely dried off and most times just tossed his clothing on, still dripping wet. He had done it for as long as Wick could remember and it had always bothered him.

Dagger just watched Wick closely. He thought he was paying too much attention to making sure he was dry. It was a waste of time, according to Dagger. He didn't see the need.

Wick helped him out of the bathroom because he was still wobbly on his feet and he really didn't want Dagger to fall. Wick struggled to get him into some boxers. They fought and argued about getting them on so much that Wick let out a grunt of frustration. Dagger just wanted to sleep without them. He said it was just so much nicer and comfortable to sleep that way. Wick did not agree with this as he glared at Dagger, the boxers still in his hand.

Wick was fed up with Dagger and this behavior of his. He was being terribly unreasonable. They had fought well over half an hour about getting boxers on him. He refused, still stating all his reasons for why he just couldn't wear the boxers.

Wick finally gave up, and all but threw his lover back onto the bed after he pulled the sheets back, making sure he wouldn't have to move him again to tuck him in. Once his lover was settled in the bed, Wick left the room. He would come back and lay down beside his lover once he was sure that he was out cold. But honestly, first, he needed some time to calm down, so he didn't murder his guardian for his terrible judgement and behaviour tonight. He was beyond frustrated with the behavior that Dagger had shown him. Dagger was stubborn in his ways, and Wick knew when to drop it. Dagger was safe and tucked in the bed where he belonged.

Wick headed downstairs to get started on the full mess that his guardian had created. He wanted to call Risk and tell him about the mess he had walked in on, but he didn't. He thought it best if he just kept this one to himself. Dagger would no doubt regret getting drunk, and if he remembered the mess, it would likely embarrass him.

Looking over at the kitchen again, he shook his head at the mess. If Dagger remembered, he was going to have to really ask how he had got the sauce right up to the ceiling. It probably did in the wallpaper in the kitchen after this. If it wasn't, Wick was going to be shocked beyond belief.

Looking under the kitchen sink, Wick didn't immediately find anything that screamed use me to clean the mess. He might actually have to call Risk to ask what the best thing to use was. He took several bottles out from under the sink and attempted to use them to clean the mess. After three different products, on just the stovetop and a lot of arm power, he had cleaned the stovetop. At this rate, he would be here almost all night and he was painfully aware of that. He couldn't use his magic to help this mess, either. Using the kitchen scrubby, he wiped down the sides and front of the stove, and it wiped off pretty nicely with just a single pass. Moving on to the floor, he hunted down the mop and bucket he knew Dagger had kept around. He just really wasn't sure where.

Wick found the mop when he opened the closet off the kitchen. It was inside the bucket. He was pleased with his find. Finding the mop was the simple part. He needed to use it now to clean the floor.

Filling the bucket with hot water and cleaner, he set the bucket on the floor and made a game plan for what section of the floor he was actually going to clean first. There was just so much to do. The cleaner and the hot water combo really worked on the kitchen tiles. Wick was thankful for that. The only thing that Wick kept thinking about was that Dagger better not say he never helps out. He was doing more than helping out here; he was hiding the evidence of Dagger's dreadful night drinking. He was even making sure he didn't have to ask Risk for help, so that Dagger wasn't embarrassed.

Looking around the kitchen again, the floor and the stove were cleaned. It really made a dent in the look of the red sauced room. It was finally looking almost normal, besides the ceiling, fridge, counters, table where Dagger had slept, and the plethora of countertop appliances that Dagger rarely used.

Sighing, Wick grabbed the fridge cleaner and prayed to the fates that this would be just as easy as the floor tiles and the stove to clean. Somehow, he had a feeling that it would not be that simple and he was going to have to work to get the fridge clean.

Wick had been right when he thought about that. Scrubbing at the fridge with another scrubby, he wanted to just coat the thing in all the different cleaners and wait for something to happen. It might melt or come clean. Either way, then, it was dealt with as far as he was concerned.

Deciding that Dagger might be really mad if he melted the fridge, he went back to scrubbing the holy heavens out of the fridge. He hoped with his arm strength the mess would come clean, and it did. A long while later, and after a few minutes of sitting with cleaner on it. He didn't waste any time on the counters. The cleaner he used was the same one he used on the fridge. He went and cleaned all the small appliances. The toaster was the worst of all the small appliances. There was no way Wick was going to get that poor thing cleaned. It was headed for the trash. At least he knew what he could buy Dagger for his birthday now. Along with a few other things.

Setting the toaster aside for the trash, he gave the counters a good wipe, and the cleaner peeled the sauce off with no problems. God, was Wick ever thankful for that. That had been the job with the most space to clean.

The ceiling and walls plus the table were the only things that were left, and it was late. Wick hoped and prayed he would at least get to sleep in after all this. If he didn't, he was going to be cranky later.

Not wanting anything to strip Dagger's prized kitchen table, Wick only used soap and water to clean the tabletop after he got everything removed from the top. Scrubbing at the spot where Dagger had sat, he was slowly getting the mess off the table. He had a towel set on the chair so he could wipe up the extra water. If he left watermarks on the table, Dagger would be livid and he would never hear the end.

The ceiling and the walls were the last things to do. But Wick needed a break, so he sat down and stared at the ceiling, trying to figure out how he was going to clean the gosh darn ceiling. There had to be away.

Wick finally settled on just standing on a kitchen chair and scrubbing the ceiling till it came clean. If it was stained, Dagger could paint it again some other time. Pulling the chair to where he needed it, he climbed on the chair and was happy he could reach the ceiling as he cleaned. It was a lot of work, but he got the ceiling cleaned. The wall was the last thing to do. Then he was in the home stretch and could head to bed.

He was really just craving sleep at this point. He even debated just leaving the wall for tomorrow, but he knew Dagger wouldn't want to see it. Hell, even he didn't want to see it tomorrow. Stretching his arms and back before he pushed the chair in and got down on the floor to be able to scrub the wall, Wick was glad he was a Skorwn now and not human or this would have taken him far longer than it already had.

Finishing the wall didn't come soon enough for Wick, who tossed all the dirty scrubby's in the trash, along with the toaster when he was finished. He put everything back where it belonged, that included all the cleaners, and flicked off the light. He headed upstairs to his room to get changed before crawling into Dagger's bed with him for a well-deserved night's rest.

10 - Chapter Ten -

When Dagger woke up, the sun was barely out and his head was splitting. He knew the wine had caused the pain. He wasn't an idiot, at least not fully an idiot. Glancing over, Wick was laid out on the bed. He was sound asleep. He was on top of the covers, which meant he totally was naked under the blankets, just like he had remembered. Bits and pieces from the red sauce mistake came back in waves of pain. This was why Dagger didn't drink ever. Glancing at his ward, he listened to the way he was breathing. It was comforting to not only hear his breath but also his heart beating steadily in the silence of the dark bedroom. Once Dagger was sure Wick was still deeply sleeping and wouldn't wake up for a bit, he crawled closer and laid against his back. He wanted the comfort of his beloved partner to ease some of his pain. He could hear and feel Wick's heart beating even better now where he laid his head. It was super soothing to hear his heart this close. Wick's back was super warm and Dagger found himself pretty rapidly falling back asleep, even if he hadn't wanted to. He snuggled deeper into Wick and closed his eyes. There was no way he was going to be able to stay awake.

Dagger woke up again at ten am, still cuddled to Wick's back like he had been earlier. Wick hadn't moved an inch since Dagger cuddled against him. Carefully, he moved away from his animus. He didn't want to wake him up accidentally. Slipping out of the bed, he pulled on a random pair of boxers and a t-shirt. This was acceptable because they weren't supposed to have any visitors today. He was also pretty sure he was going to be cleaning the kitchen for months. Quietly, he stalked to the kitchen, expecting the largest mess he'd ever seen, but his kitchen was perfectly clean and in working order. There was not one spot of sauce anywhere, which confused him for a moment. He knew that left only one person to clean his mess because he didn't. He felt bad right away and also knew that's why Wick was still sleeping. Wick had probably worked half the night getting the kitchen cleaned. Dagger felt super guilty that he was the reason Wick still needed rest, and a lot of it. From the flashes he got, the kitchen had been terrible.

Dagger let his animus sleep. He didn't have the heart to wake him for anything, not after seeing the kitchen. In the time his animus slept, he went out and got groceries, bought a treat for Wick and bought more lounge clothing for him as well. Wick would be more grateful for more lounge clothing. He found them comfortable and in his size.

When Dagger got back, Wick was still sound asleep. Figuring his ward would wake up in the next few hours, he put dinner on in the slow cooker and it was well past three in the afternoon before Dagger even saw Wick up and moving, not that he was surprised. His animus hunted down a hot cup of coffee, drinking down the contents of the first cup. Armed with a second cup, Wick went to find Dagger. Wick was carrying his cup of coffee like a war trophy. It shocked Dagger to see him drinking coffee this late, but he knew why.

Dagger couldn't help but feel his beloved partner was pissed at him about the drinking. Hell, even Dagger was mad at himself for his behavior when he was drinking, but it wasn't just Dagger assuming that Wick was furious.

Dagger was getting glared at over the edge of the coffee cup that rested like treasure between his hands. Wick was slowly taking sips out of the cup.

"I'm really sorry. I thought that was a good idea—-"

Dagger saw Wick raise his hand to stop him from speaking as he continued to sip at the mug before he finished his coffee. As Wick's coffee cup touched the tabletop again, Wick spoke and oh boy, was he livid. His anger laced his tone with coldness and Dagger knew Wick was more the right here. He didn't even have to think about it.

"That was very dangerous. You could have burned down the house. You completely passed out when I came back. Please never do that again."

"I really didn't mean to—-"

"I'm not done talking yet, Dagger."

"Oh, My bad. Please continue."

"Now, back to what I was saying. You passed out, and the stove was still on. Not to mention the kitchen looked like a red sauce bomb went off in here. Care to explain that? Or how the hell you got red sauce on the damn ceiling, it was well above the pot and your head."

Dagger rubbed the back of his neck, attempting to recall that part of the night. Surprised, he found he actually remembered that part. As his mind replayed him putting the jar in the boiling water, he flinched. Why the hell had he put a frozen jar of tomato sauce in the pot and let it boil? He really was not that stupid normally! Dagger bunched up all his words as he spits them out quickly so he would have to say anything else. Wick didn't need to know about his stupid mistake.

Despite the fact that Dagger had mashed all his words together, Wick still understood everything he said. That just made Wick's rant all the more true about it being dangerous. In what was quickly becoming their fashion, they fought. The difference was Wick didn't feel angry at Dagger. With each word they seemed to yell at each other, the sexual energy in the room rose until Dagger just random yelled out for Wick to kiss him. Wick wasn't sure his ears were hearing what his brain thought it had heard.

"What?" He deadpanned.

"Kiss me."

Wick didn't wait any longer. He walked around the island and backed Dagger into the corner. He was pressed flush against Dagger when their lips met. There was no denying what Dagger felt, because Wick felt all of Dagger's excitement. When they finally pulled back from each other, they were both breathing roughly and taking in deep breaths. Dagger struggled to pull as much air in as he had deprived himself with the kiss.

Dagger couldn't believe how much the kid he once called little and cute had grown up. The man in front of him was something he had to be neglecting to see. He had been so blind he didn't see Wick for what he was. A grown man.

This man was stunningly handsome. Dagger could admire him for hours. Some sense of sick pride filled his gut that he could raise and now have this man. It made Dagger slightly sick. That he had that thought. Regardless, Dagger ran his hand through his animus's hair. The wavy blond mess gave him a surfer's ocean styled hair and Dagger both hated and loved the mess that it was. The softness, however, spoke a much different story. He looked after his hair very well. Most times, he had it wrapped up in a bun. Dagger grabbed the male's chin and pulled him down for another kiss. A small part of him said this was wrong, a much larger part of him told him this was right, oh so very right. At this moment, he didn't care which side was the truth. He only cared about the kiss he was sharing with his long sought after beloved.

Pulling back from the kiss, Dagger looked over Wick again. He wondered what person Wick's father was. His birth father. After all, it was where Wick had got all his looks.

"Wick, do you think you would ever like to know who your father is?"

"No. Not really. I have Risk. Why do I need another father?"

"It would help you know where you come from."

"I don't care where I come from, just like I don't care about what family status I hold."

"I think you should ask the next time you go for a check-up."

"You are trying to push me to do something I don't want to do . I am happy with the way things are now and I have a father. Risk is my father for all intents and purposes. Just leave it at that."

"Wick, you cannot just shut me down like that. I raised you."

"You and Risk, you both raised me."

Dagger knew that was true. But it didn't stop the comment from making him feel uncomfortable. It was the second time Wick had said something like that to him.

Dagger only nodded once to what Wick had said and decided to himself that if Wick wanted anything to do with his birth father, he could find him on his own.

Dagger took Wick's coffee cup off the table and walked into the kitchen. He washed the cup, setting it on the dish rack to dry. He almost wished Wick would have left him in the kitchen to clean. At least then, he would have something he could mindlessly do.

11 - Chapter Eleven -

Dagger dreaded the day that it was his birthday. He hated it because of a lot of things. A few of them were just, he was getting older; he had celebrated it way too many times, and he really didn't enjoy his birthday in a very long time. But then there was the fact that Wick really had yet to live, but Dagger had. Wick had brought him a gift but wouldn't give it to him until after breakfast, when he told Dagger to remain in bed. Dagger was brooding over what he was going to do today. There were plenty of things he could do today, But he had to make time for his father and everyone else that would invade his home in just a few hours.

Wick returned sometime later with a tray of food. There were two plates on it and two forks. Dagger smiled to himself. Wick had made them breakfast. Though he wasn't really fond of them in the bed part, he would let it slide. For today.

Dagger admired the cooking that his ward had done. Waffles, eggs and bacon, hash browns and fresh strawberries, all looked so good. His mouth was watering just looking at it. Wick made sure he had brought a damp dish towel and napkins for them both. Without even having to ask, Wick had placed the tray on Dagger's lap and went around the bed, climbing up on the other side.

"I've made a massive selection. I hope this is all ok?"

"Oh god yeah, it's more than ok, those waffles look divine."

"I thought you would be over the moon about the waffles you always are."

Dagger paused and looked at Wick. He wasn't really sure how to answer that, but he tried.

"Am I? I never realized I was over the moon about waffles. I really enjoy them though, but over the moon, haha, you don't think that's a stretch?"

"No, Absolutely not, I've seen you devour waffles quickly. You have done it since I was a young boy."

"You remember too much from your childhood, ha."

"I was an only child. I had a lot of time to watch people."

"Right, I should have had more cousins around."

"They tried to come over, If I remember correctly, but you wouldn't let them too much. You didn't like that they dirtied the house every time they came over, and they were loud."

"Ah, yes. I remember that. They were so damn loud and bouncy. You were always so quiet."

Wick smiled as he took his plate off the tray and let Dagger have the tray. He knew Dagger would be grateful to have the tray. Dagger sliced into his waffles first and savored the first bite. He enjoyed it immensely. The perfect amount of butter and syrup had been added and allowed to melt. It moved Dagger to savor every single bite. The waffles had been the best part of the breakfast and he was pleased with Wick's ability to cook.

"Are your waffles up to your liking?"

"Shush, I'm savoring my delicious waffles."

"Oh, are you?"

"Shush, more chew, less talk."

Dagger went back to munching on his waffles, and he was really enjoying them. Once he had cleared his waffles, he munched the bacon that Wick placed on his plate for him. Dagger really wasn't a fan of bacon, but it really was going down well and he was loving the saltiness of the bacon. Wick handed him a glass of water. Dagger just looked at the water. He was wondering where the coffee was and Wick looked a little guilty about something.

"Where is the coffee?"

"You can't have coffee today."

"Why not?"

"So, I broke the coffee pot and now we may not have coffee with breakfast."

"You broke the coffee pot, How?"

"Honestly, I'm not sure, But it smelt pretty burnt and nasty."

"You broke my coffee pot on my birthday, is that right?"

"Yes, that is right."

"You better tell Risk to pick me up a new coffee pot on his way over here or I'm going to die from lack of caffeine."

"You will not die from lack of caffeine, you will be just fine, just eat your hash browns and suck it up."

"I will surely die from lack of caffeine, and then what will you do, huh?"

"Nothing, because you will be more than fine. You are being pretty dramatic about this. It's just coffee."

"Just coffee, you say, but it is my lifeblood. I need it to live."

"You are still so dramatic for your age."

"It is my birthday. I am allowed."

Dagger ignored him, stuffing a giant bite of the hash brown into his mouth and loving he could taste the onion in the hash browns. He had ketchup to dip his hash browns in, but he didn't. The plain ketchup free hash browns were a really delicious thing today. They were going down very well and Dagger would have to ask Wick when they were both finished if there were more hash browns. Dagger hoped Wick had made more, he really hoped. But he would take more waffles too if there were more.

Dagger and Wick finished their breakfast in silence, both too busy chewing to speak, and the silence was a comfortable one. Wick took their plates down to the dishwasher and rinsed everything before loading it, tossing a soap puck in and turning it on.

When Wick returned to the bedroom, Dagger hadn't moved a mere inch out of the bed. He was in the same spot he was when Wick left, but had relaxed and stretched out.

"Dagger, I know from what we planned that family will come after one. They want to have a cake and have you open gifts. They have planned for dinner. I am in the dark on what restaurant they plan to go to, but I'm positive Risk will let us know."

"Do we have to do anything for it? I would much rather just lay in bed with you all day long. There is nothing else I want."

"You know that would never fly with Risk. He will not allow you to sleep on your birthday, he never has. Be prepared to have all the birthday fixings."

"I know. That's what I'm afraid of. I just want to lie in bed and sleep. I don't want to celebrate it. You would think he would grow tired of celebrating my birthday by now."

"You know that would never happen. He loves you and wants you to have a great day."

"Please, he might love me and my brothers, but that man adores you and he always has Wick. He has always demanded you have the same, if not more, than my siblings and I."

"Yeah,"

"On a serious note, Wick, I knew I could never fill the role as even a replacement father. It just wasn't something I could do. Raise you. I could do that, but parent you completely, I could have never. Risk took over for things I could not do for you and I'm grateful you two have a bond the way you do. Risk didn't care about offending anyone by being a father to you. He saw you needed a father, and he took that job and role. In the beginning, there were many nights where I couldn't do it and I needed help. He was there for us both when we needed him."

"Oh, Dagger, I know. Risk helped us both. Being a father was natural for him. He saw I needed a father, and he took that role. Though since the start of my teenage years, he has pulled back on his fatherly behavior. Which saddens me deeply. I still appreciate that he is there for me so much. Don't get me wrong, When it comes to raising me you did a lot of the work but for emotional parenting, that's where Risk was."

"Trust me, I was never happier than to share raising you with him. He picked up in every spot I faltered, all well helping me heal, too. I wouldn't, for a minute, change how things happen to raise you."

"Really?"

"There might be one thing I would change?"

"And what exactly is that?"

"I would tell off Prodigy for everything. I would make that male understand he is just a guest in your life and doesn't have to be there. I would speak my mind to him."

"You still can, you know, you don't have to 'go back' to do

it."

"You are an adult now. It's your job to tell him how you want to be treated."

"But you are my beloved partner. It is also your right to tell him how I should be treated, and I think one day you will. One day you will grow tired of his games, much like I have and you will tell him where to go and how to get there and when you do, it will be worth it."

12 - Chapter Twelve -

Risk showed up alone, just an hour later. With him, he brought a cake and presents, along with a new coffee pot, which both Wick and Dagger called and texted for him to pick up from the store.

Dagger and Wick were in the living room, lounging back on the couch, just watching movies, and eating chocolate chips, right out of the bag.

"I see you two will never change, on the couch eating chocolate chips together."

Wick and Dagger both looked at him. They had been too wrapped up in their movie to know that Risk had just walked right in.

"I never even heard you come in. Did you bring the coffee pot?"

"You will find that on the counter, ready to come out of the box and be set up."

"Hell yeah, I need coffee." Wick declared, abandoning his spot on the couch.

Risk sat down on the couch and leaned sideways into Dagger until he had his attention. Dagger looked at his father, trying to hide the smile on his face as he spoke.

"Can I help you with something?"

"Oh, I think you can."

"And what would that be?"

"You could pause your movie and give me a hug."

"Alright, sounds fair."

Dagger paused the movie and let his father hug him, hugging him back gently, But Risk didn't let go when Dagger did. His father was going to suck up this hug. He couldn't remember the last time they had embraced this way.

"I don't think I've told you enough how proud of you I am. You raised a boy that didn't have a chance in hell without you. He turned out so good and will be a great man. You have found your beloved partner, though I know the circumstances of it are a little hard to swallow. And you're finally happy again. I couldn't be happier for you and about you, Dagger."

Dagger's heart clenched at his father's words. He wrapped his arms around his dad again, giving him another powerful hug. When they both pulled back, they said no other words. Instead, Dagger headed to the kitchen to get some of the coffee he could now smell. Risk was right on his heels. Wick was watching the coffeemaker and holding a mug in his hands, Dagger smiled to himself again. His ward looked pleased to have coffee in just a few minutes. Dagger also felt that way. He needed some coffee.

"So, What would you like to do for your birthday dinner? Do you have a place in mind?"

"I will go anywhere Dagger chooses, I'm not picky."

Dagger thought about it. Was there really anywhere he wanted to go out and eat? He would have to dress in his robes if they went anywhere fancy and Wick would have to wear the black robes now that he awakened and he would hate that.

"We could go anywhere, but mandatory robe restaurants. Wick has his proper robes, but as you know, he doesn't like them."

Wick turned to Dagger, his eyes slightly wide, and he spoke with a touch of annoyance in his tone.

"I would wear it if I had to. All you have to do is ask."

"Wick, I am not about to make you uncomfortable so that we can have dinner. We have plenty of other options."

"No. We will go somewhere fancy. You deserve to have it. I'll dress in the black robes. Besides, there's a new place that opened that you wanted to try."

"Oh, yes, that sounds like a fantastic idea. Dagger, You have the final say of course,"

Dagger looked at Risk. He was weighing the options in his head and the biggest one was just calling the whole thing off and getting back into bed. He knew he would disappoint both Wick and his father, but he really wasn't feeling it.

"I think maybe..."

"Don't give Dagger the last choice. He will choose to stay home and go back to bed. You know he isn't fond of his birthdays. We go through it every year."

"That isn't an option here. We will be going out for dinner, one way or another."

"I don't have a choice about what I want to do for my birthday?"

"Not this part of your birthday Dagger, I know how you are with your birthday." Risk said, looking Dagger right in the eye, giving him a look that said he would not be taking Dagger's crap behavior today.

"Fine, We can go for dinner. The place that Wick mentioned is fine."

"Good, Good. Your brothers are going to meet us there and then come back here for cake and ice cream."

"Who all did you invite to invade my home?"

"Just the regular family."

"So, like everyone then, sounds about right."

"You are being dramatic again, Dagger." Wick said, pouring his own cup of coffee, to which Dagger took it right out of his hand and sipped it.

"That was mine."

"You were too busy giving me backtalk to enjoy it."

Risk just sighed as he poured Wick another coffee before he poured one for himself.

"So, what are your plans until dinnertime?"

"Is sleeping a proper option?"

"You can nap if you would like. I still have a few more things to do. I should be back in a couple of hours."

"Alright, sounds good."

Risk left, and Wick looked at Dagger, before heading upstairs and then making his way back down again. He had a gift bag in his hand and looked at the Dagger with a smile.

"I bought you a couple of things. I wasn't sure what to actually buy you, so I bought you many things that made me think of you."

Dagger and Wick headed to the living room where Dagger sat down and Wick handed him the gift bag. Pulling out the first box, he unwrapped it and laughed. It was a toaster, a super fancy one.

"Thank you for the toaster, and for cleaning the kitchen a few weeks ago after the drinking mistake."

"Hey, no worries, you would have spent hours cleaning it and it would have been harder to clean then. It didn't take too long anyway,"

Pulling the second box out of the bag, Dagger unwrapped the smaller box and quickly realized it was a jewelry box. He held the box in his hands and looked at Wick.

"Open it. I promise you will like it."

"Wick, you don't have to spend this kind of money on me."

"You don't even know what it is, just open it."

Dagger sighed and opened the box. The watch in the box was stunning. The look of it shocked Dagger. It had beautiful leather bands and silver parts with gold accents. Dagger knew this thing was not cheap. He felt bad Wick had spent that amount of money on him. There were plenty of other things he could have spent that money on.

"Let me put it on you."

"Wick, I do like it, but why?"

"I saw it and thought it would be perfect for you."

"Oh, Wick, you could have bought me a single cupcake with a candle or hand made me a card as you used to when you were a small boy and it would have been enough."

"I wanted you to have something really nice from me, that's why."

"I do have something really nice from you already, your time."

"That is really cheesy, and it makes me happy to hear that, but I needed to buy you something nice for once."

"May I put it on you?"

"I suppose so, but I will feel terrible if I break it."

"Don't worry too much about that. I have a coverage plan because accidents happen."

Wick took the watch out of the box and Dagger saw there was an inscription on the back, but he didn't catch what the watch said, But he still let him place it on his arm. Dagger looked at the watch on his arm and smiled.

"Can I have a hug?"

"You never have to ask for a hug, Dagger, just hug me."

Dagger stood up and hugged Wick. When he pulled away from Wick, he kissed the male's forehead.

"What was that for?"

"I was showing my appreciation."

"I see. You still have more gifts to open."

"Oh, Ok."

Dagger reached back into the bag and pulled out a really nice sweater and a new pair of robes. He frowned at seeing the black color. He couldn't wear black robes, Wick had to know that.

"I appreciate the robes. They are nicely made but I can't wear them. I am not allowed."

"They are not for right now, but for some point in the future."

"Wick, I am confused."

"Good, stay that way until you need those robes, besides the ones in the closet need to be replaced."

Dagger understood the robes then. They were for after they mated; it was a Skorwn tradition. A merging of families, you could say. He wondered if Risk had known about this and that was why he had left so that they could have some alone time together. Dagger felt his heart flutter, and he looked at Wick, smiling at him.

"Thank you."

13 - Chapter Thirteen -

Risk showed up a few hours later and demanded the boys get ready for dinner. Dagger was still tired. His father had woken him up from a pretty good sleep. He had fallen asleep on the couch, leaned against Wick's shoulder after they had watched tv for a little and did some lighthearted fooling around.

Wick helped Dagger get dressed into a white robe from the closet before heading to his own room to get a black robe set to dress in. Wick hated birthdays. He would wear the damn thing. The hope was that this night would go off with no problems and that they would be closer than before. Dagger had taken the robes well, so that was a pleasant thing.

Risk had called for a shuttle to come and pick them up. Risk inspected Wick and Dagger walking side by side and smiled to himself. They looked good together, a power couple.

Risk wondered how long it would be before they finally got the mating over with and settled into a new normal. He would be happy to see Dagger have that finally, a proper mate.

Risk felt bad for setting Dagger up with Inn, but Prodigy had begged Risk for help and support. Dagger had been on board with the idea. He had known Inn before the marriage, but they weren't friends or even acquaintances. They had just been in the same circles until Dagger had worked for the officers.

Risk knew Pyro was still very much interested in having Dagger work for him, he was reminded every time he went to speak with Pyro; they were friends after all.

Dagger looked at his father who held the door to shuttle and go inside, Wick right after him, and then his father. Dagger smoothed out his robes before doing the same to Wick's so that they didn't wrinkle.

Wick lightly grabbed his hand and brought it up to his lips. Dagger was surprised by the act and watched. Until his father looked at them. Then Dagger pulled his hand away from Wick. Wick looked at Risk, who smiled softly at them, then hardened his eyes as he gave Dagger a look. Dagger knew he was being unfair to Wick with that action, But he wasn't ready for some of the judgment that would follow.

Wick didn't care, not in the slightest. He hoped that all the high-class families would be there tonight, so he could stake his claim on Dagger and just get it over with. He was tired of Dagger being worried about what others would think about them. Out of all the people he hoped would be there, he hoped his grandfather would be in attendance, and he would get an eye full of Dagger on Wick's arm.

Risk created small talk in the car well they drove to the restaurant. Dagger was glad to see the sign come into view. He wanted to get out of the awkwardness of the car.

Being out of the car was worse. Wick took Dagger's hand in his and refused to let the male have his hand back. Dagger quickly realized why Wick had been so adamant about coming here. He wanted to show Dagger off in this manner. Dagger cast a look at his father, almost begging for help. That did little. His father just smiled at him. It was like his father was politely telling Dagger to get over it; they were beloved partners.

Dagger spotted Wick's grandfather and his ex-wife Willa having dinner. Willa spotted Dagger, and smiled, smiling further when she saw her grandson. Prodigy turned and you could see his face fall, more so when he saw Dagger's hand in Wick's. Dagger tried to pull his hand out of Wick's again, but he clenched it, not allowing him to do so.

"Wick, you are going to make a scene. Please, stop."

"You are the one making a scene, Dagger."

Dagger sighed, his shoulders dropping as he allowed Wick to drag him to a table close to his grandparents. Willa gave Dagger a sympathetic look. Prodigy spoke to Risk quietly and

Dagger didn't have to guess what they were talking about. He knew it was about Wick's behavior. Willa's eyes lit up as she conversed with Risk. Prodigys did not. His mood went somber and his voice raised from more than a whisper, allowing Dagger and Wick to hear them.

"You are telling me that my grandson is your son's beloved partner and you are well and good with this?"

"Yes, I am. It isn't my job to stand in the way of beloved partners, it isn't your job either."

"So first I am to give him my son, but now I am to give him my only grandson as well?"

Dagger felt sick. This was not how he wanted his birthday to turn out. He pulled his hand from Wick's roughly and made his way out of the restaurant and into the lobby. He wanted more than anything to go home now. Someone in black robes grabbed his arm as he sidestepped around them.

"Dagger, hello."

He looked up, meeting eyes with Pyro, the leader.

"Hey."

"You look like you have had better days."

"I have."

"Shame that someone ruined your birthday,"

"My birthday... How did you know it was my birthday?"

"Ah, I saw your father earlier. I sought to ask him something, and he went on and on about your birthday, and how proud he is of you. I've heard your ward had gone through his awakening, too. How is he?"

"Oh Pyro, That is a loaded question."

"I hear my cousin is up to nothing good since his awakening."

"That is just the beginning of it."

"Is it? Perhaps you should fill me in some time and lend a hand. I know dealing with Prodigy must not be the easiest thing for you, after everything."

"We should, I want to ask you about some——"

I felt someone grab my arm roughly. Wick was towering over me, The scent of anger rolling off of him.

"Good evening Wick. Nice to see you," Pyro said, smiling at Wick.

"Nice to see you, too. Dagger, I came to inform you that Risk and Prodigy have made a scene and I don't think we will be welcome to eat here again."

Dagger turned and looked at Wick with shock on his face.

"What happened?"

"They exchanged hands."

"They were fighting!"

"Yes. Willa and I tried to stop them, But after they wouldn't stop, she said to just let them fight it out. But I thought I should make you aware."

Dagger lost his temper right there in front of Pyro.

"This is all because you wanted to make it known that we are beloved partners. You couldn't have just waited until we were all alone and not in public!"

"Well, excuse me! I wanted to make it so that Prodigy didn't go up one side of you and down the other. My damn bad!"

Dagger stomped off and Wick would have followed, but Pyro took his arm.

"Give him time. He needs space. He has put up with a lot from Prodigy. Let's go see if we can fix the issues with Prodigy and Risk."

"Alright."

Wick couldn't argue with Pyro about what Dagger has put up with from Prodigy over all the years. If anyone knew it would be Pyro, they were cousins, after all.

Dagger hadn't got too far by stomping off and he regretted his behavior, but this was not how he wanted his night to go. He would have so much rather spent it at home, just Wick and him, where they could have talked about all this. Instead, now, many people knew what was going on and then there was the fact that his father and Prodigy had got into a fight in the middle of the restaurant. If his father had engaged in a fight with the other male, it meant he had said something about Dagger that his father just couldn't stand for a moment longer.

Dagger sighed and made his way back down to the restaurant. He needed to solve this and quickly, before all this happened again. Wick and Pyro were not on the stairs when he returned, but Willa was there instead. She smiled when she saw Dagger again.

"I knew you would come back. You always did."

"I'm sorry."

"No, I'm sorry Dagger, You didn't deserve to spend your birthday like this, and Prodigy needs to respect boundaries and understand that he doesn't have a choice of who and what Wick does. He is a grown man. There was a reason our grandson went to you and not to him and me. It was because Risk and you were the best options for him. I am quite happy you two are beloved partners. You deserve happiness, too. And not false happiness."

"Where are they?"

"Pyro and Wick took them to another room, a private room, to talk over their issues. Pyro is in the room with those three to make sure they don't murder each other. I came to wait for you."

"This is all so stressful. When I found out Wick was my beloved partner, I knew things would be rough, but I didn't expect this."

"Prodigy said something tonight that should have never left his mouth and will never leave mine. But he deserved everything your father gave him. For your father to hit him, that should say enough. We know your father for his kindness. Let me just tell you, I am glad I am not married to Prodigy any longer."

"I feel terrible."

"Oh honey, you have nothing to feel terrible about. If anyone should feel terrible, it is Prodigy and I hope he feels terrible. What happened here tonight should have never happened. Moving on to a far nicer subject, When you decide if you and Wick are going to have a ceremony, let me know, I would like to be the one to make you both official in the ceremony. I would give anything to cover Inn's name in that book."

"I appreciate the offer. I'm not sure what we will do. We are not even bonded."

"Stop waiting. Inn would not be mad about this. You know how bad he wanted you to find someone else, he wanted you to be happy. He felt bad you were in the same trap he was."

"But for me, it didn't feel like a trap. I was happy knowing he could confide in me until he couldn't."

"Oh Dagger, that wasn't your fault. Inn is the one to blame. He would have never blamed you for any of this, not for a moment."

"Should we find them and see what is going on?"

"Perhaps, who knows what they have said or done now? Maybe they have all calmed down."

"I doubt it. This is Prodigy we are speaking of, he doesn't have a calm. He has two moods, Mad and entitled."

"I wish you were wrong about that, sadly you are not."

Willa and Dagger headed back inside, and they walked to a private room. Opening the door, Pyro was holding back Wick and Prodigy. They both looked like they might attack each other again.

"Please, relax both of you. I understand both your feelings right now, but it would be better to talk this out than to attack each other."

Dagger frowned at Wick, who backed off, seeing the look on Dagger's face. He made his choice then that fighting with Dagger was not a wise option. He went and sat on one of the lounge chairs. Pyro looked at Dagger with thankfulness in his eyes.

"Prodigy, we need to have a long-overdue conversation. You're not going to like what we talk about either, but it needs to be said. This, here, it can't go on any longer." Dagger said in a very commanding tone, one Wick was sure he had never heard come from Dagger before. This had to be his all-business tone.

14 - Chapter Fourteen -

Every bonded set of Skorwn had bonding tattoos, but it was not something that they taught you, usually because the tattoos were in a spot you didn't just go showing off. Wick's tattoo was over his right peck and right down his ribs. It was a beautiful tribal piece. Daggers was all the way from his finger up his arm, right to pretty much his whole shoulder.

Dagger still couldn't believe that after he had given Prodigy a piece of his mind in front of everyone that Wick would have been as turned on as he was. After that, they had all come back to Dagger's home and ordered takeout. Dagger had been thankful that his brothers had been held up with other things and didn't have to witness what had gone down. They had made it for takeout and cake and ice cream, though.

When they finally left, Dagger didn't expect Wick to go cave dweller on him as he had. Dagger didn't stop Wick when he could have either, he let Wick ravage his body until it came down to doing the deed. Wick had taken on for the team last night, and Dagger had been the one to take him.

Dagger looked at the black tattoo all over his arm and hand.

How was he going to hide it when he went into public? The thing was massive! The tattoo was amazing, though. He had seen Wicks when he woke up, but made no move to wake him up to show him. There was plenty of time for that later. Sipping his coffee, Dagger never heard his father let himself in. Instead, Dagger got the shit scared out of him when his father said good morning. He wasn't expecting his father to be here.

Risk's eyes locked right onto the tattoo on his son's hand. He knew right away what it was. Sniffing the air, he chuckled.

"You could have showered. You have an odor."

"I needed coffee, and I am all too aware I smell like stale sex."

"You smell like a brothel."

"Thank you. That's very kind."

"You know me, I'm always kind."

"I keep hearing that, but I'm not sure we are all talking about the same man."

Risk sipped the coffee he took from the coffee-pot and waited till Dagger had his full cup of coffee gone and was working on the second before he asked about the tattoo on his hand.

"So, Your hand, huh? How'd that happen?"

"Wick and I were fooling around after our breakfast yesterday morning before you showed up.

He bit my finger. I didn't even think about it until I woke up and saw my arm and hand. It goes up pretty far."

"Oh, So when you guys had sex last night you didn't need to bite each other because there were still fresh marks. So you didn't have the urge to mark him?"

"No, not really, because I bit him when we were fooling around right before the sex. Now, are you done knowing about my sex life? Geez, dad, go ask my brothers about theirs."

"You're mighty cranky this morning. Did you need a pain pill?"

Dagger couldn't keep the sick smile off his face as he turned to face his father. He felt bad about the words coming out of his mouth.

"Nope, I am pain-free."

Dagger watched his father's face drop as he seemed to put Dagger's words together before he sipped his coffee and mumbled the words 'Poor Kid.' Dagger shrugged his shoulders.

"I was pretty gentle with him, all things considered."

"Dagger!"

"What, you wanted to know so much before?"

"Dagger, I really hope you went easy on him. That might have been his first time."

Dagger's face went red as he remembered walking in a Wick

and another male.

"I can promise you, that was not his first time. Just his first time as an awakened Skorwn."

"Dagger, how do you know that?"

"I saw some shit, ok. Accidents happen when you are raising a teenage boy."

"You caught him in the act!"

"Shut up, don't say that too loud! It was a few years ago and I swear, I don't want to talk about it anymore."

"I am not sure who I should feel bad for, you or him."

"I just know. It's not nice being on both sides of the event."

"I remember catching you."

"Oh, I remember too. Trust me."

Wick woke up around noon and he could hear his male downstairs talking to another, whom he presumed was Risk. He groaned at the pain in his ass. Gosh, Dagger had some snappy hips. He wasn't regretting letting Dagger have him that way last night.

Turning over towards the nightstand, he smiled to himself when he noticed the water and the bottle of pain pills. Dagger had made sure he was taken care of. Taking the pills, he laid in bed till some of the pain subsided. When he got up, he moved to shower and shave. His eyes fell on the large tattoo that took up most of his right side. He looked at the thing in the mirror; it was eye-catching, and he wanted to make sure Dagger got a good look at the thing. It was proof of what they had done last night.

Slipping on boxers and lounge pants, he made his way down the stairs and into the kitchen. There was a beautiful set of marks on Dagger's arm as far up as he could see. He wobbled to the sweet coffee he could smell coming from the pot. He desperately wanted a cup.

"When did the marks show up?"

"I woke up with it."

"So then it's safe to assume we got them overnight? After everything."

"I would think so."

Risk wouldn't look Wick in the eyes and Wick had a strange feeling that Risk knew he was the one who took the position of the bottom last night. Risk said nothing to him, though, not that he would, because Risk didn't judge any of his children or their spouses.

Risk felt for Wick. Dagger definitely hadn't been as light on him as he had said he was. Wick had bruises along his hips that Risk hadn't meant to see but had when he grabbed a cup out of the cupboard.

"Dagger, those are some bruises you left."

Wick turned to look down at his hips and blinked before looking at Risk.

"That would make sense why my damn hips are tender."

"No, your hips are tender because I beat on them." Dagger snickered.

"Dagger, be respectful." Risk said softly.

"I was."

"You were not."

"When did you even get here?" Wick asked, yawning.

"I got here a while ago. Dagger had asked me to come for breakfast last night and then he wasn't even awake, so I waited for him and scared him at the same time."

"Shoot! I asked you to come for breakfast, didn't I?"

"Yes, you did."

Dagger set his coffee down and stretched again before going to see what he had for groceries in the fridge. He knew he needed to go shopping, but he hadn't done it yet. Dagger felt Wick's eyes on him as he moved around the kitchen and was fighting the urge to tell him to stop staring at him. But he didn't. Instead, he turned around.

"Do you need something, Wick?"

"No, not at all."

Dagger went back to what he was doing and listened to what his father and Wick were talking about. They were quietly discussing last night when Dagger ripped into Prodigy about his terrible behavior and how he was ashamed of all the others who had to wear and be in the same family as him. Dagger felt bad about some of his word choice, but it had to be said they were once again family now.

"Dagger, Pyro asked me to speak to you and find out if you had some free time this week. He wanted to speak to you about coming back to work and having an opening for you, if you were interested."

"I'll see what I'm doing and then call him and I'll think about his offer. I'm not sure if I want to go back to work right now."

"Work would be good for you, you haven't had time like that to yourself in a long time, well before I was born."

"Speaking of work, time and things. Now that you have awakened, what do you want to do with your time?"

"Risk offered me a job working alongside him at the office. I might take him up on that. Pyro has also offered me a position working alongside my grandmother. Then there is Prodigy, who has also offered me a position at his company, though I am not sure I could handle him all that time. He is not desirable to be around."

"The choice is yours. Do what you want to, Wick."

Dagger cooked breakfast for them all, Eggs, bacon and fried potatoes. They chatted and ate. Dagger looked at Wick again, and at the mark that ran down his chest. He thanked the fates and Inn.

15 - Chapter Fifteen -

Dagger made an appointment to see Pyro today. The male had even cleared his day for Dagger to come to see him. He felt a little bad about the fact that Willa would have to move all the things he had done away with. Dagger tried to dress in his white robe, but Wick had canceled that plan right then and there. He, against Dagger's will, had dressed him in the black robe he had bought him.

"You're allowed to wear this now, we are mated."

"Doesn't mean I have to."

"If I have to, then so do you."

"I feel like a dick just wearing it."

"Don't worry, you won't turn into a Prodigy after one time wearing it."

Dagger and Wick hadn't really gone anywhere since they had

mated, so no one besides Dagger's family knew about the mating and the marks. Hell, Dagger hadn't even told Willa they had mated. He would today when he saw her, of course. She deserved to know they mated.

"What will I say if I run into Prodigy there?"

"You don't have to say a damn thing to him. Rather, I would like it if you didn't. He doesn't deserve to speak to you."

"Wick, that is your grandfather."

"He is an ass."

"That doesn't matter. He is still your grandfather."

"And what would you have me do, Dagger? Try to reason with the man? Try to connect with him?"

"You could do both of those things. They might help."

"Somehow I doubt that."

"Just give it a thought, OK?"

"I will, for you."

"I appreciate that."

Wick hugged Dagger and kissed his temple. Wick had been doing that every day now since they had mated. It comforted Dagger in a way he didn't expect. Dagger put on some ankle boots and hugged Wick once more before he headed out. Dagger wasn't too worried about Wick, he was supposed to be going to see Risk and then they were going to do something. He hadn't really listened to what they had planned. He was too busy speaking with Pyro.

Dagger was a few minutes early when he got to Pyro's office. Heading inside, he spotted Inn's older brother, Wicks uncle, who gave him a soft wave and a smile. He had always been respectful to Dagger.

Dagger knew if he was around, so was his father. He had expected to be ignored by Wick's uncle, but it seemed he couldn't get that lucky.

"Hey Dagger, how are you? I see you and Wick have mated then?"

"Yes, a little while ago."

"Many congratulations. Make sure you tell Mom. she will want to know that, of course."

"Oh, I will, When I head up to see Pyro."

"Be careful. My father is up there now. He is ranting to Pyro about company issues, and I'm sure about the fact that Wick called him late last night."

"Wick called him late last night?"

"Yes, I assumed you knew he was calling to tell his grandfather that he was turning down the job in the family company,"

"No, I did not know. He never even told me this morning when I saw him."

"Oh. Well."

"I'm not worried about it. Wick is a grown man and can make his own choices on what he would like to do."

"Word is, he chose to work with your father and Pyro."

"I was unaware that my father and Pyro were working on anything together."

"A bunch of really pleasant buildings, from what I've heard from mom."

"Oh, we could use them, I'm sure. Pyro is very picky about what he wants to build."

Dagger looked down at his watch and back at Inn's older brother.

"Excuse me, we will have to catch up again soon. I have to head in before I'm late for my meeting with Pyro."

"Yes, for sure. Have a pleasant day, Dagger."

"You too!"

Dagger walked a little faster than he had before inside the building. He knew where Pyro's office was; he had been there before. Dagger got on the only elevator and rode up to Pyro's floor.

Prodigy was waiting for the elevator when Dagger got to the top floor. He debated passing him, but Prodigy spoke to him.

"Could I have a moment of your time, Dagger?"

"A moment, yes, otherwise whatever you need will have to wait. I have a meeting with Pyro."

"I see you are wearing black robes, so you have mated with Wick then?"

"Yes, we have mated."

"Alright."

Prodigy got into the elevator and let the doors close. Dagger was surprised by how almost nice he had been about the whole thing. He wasn't surprised either that Wick hadn't told him last night when they spoke that he and Dagger were mated.

Heading into Pyro's main office, Willa saw Dagger, her eyes wide and her smile wider.

"Let me see it, I want to see your mating mark."

Dagger pulled up the black robes as far as he could to show her the mark and she hugged him with all her strength.

"Oh, I'm so happy for you. Though I'm not fond of the black robes on you, they reminded me too much of Prodigy and his pompous behavior."

"Glad we think the same thing. I think your oldest son and Pyro are the only black-robed first family members I don't think are dicks when it comes to males."

"You are not wrong. My grandson seems to have some of Prodigy's behavior too, but not the same way."

"They are both stubborn and set in one way, their own."

"Isn't that the truth?"

"I heard Wick turned down working for Prodigy in the name of working for Pyro and my father."

"Oh yes, splendid isn't it?"

"I'm sure Prodigy doesn't think so."

"When his own beloved partner comes along, he will have to change or he will have problems there. There is still hope he will find his beloved."

"I hope he changes. He is losing a relationship with his grandson because he can't let go of the sins of his son. That isn't Wick's fault."

"Prodigy is set in his ways. That's why we divorced and are nothing more than friends who share children."

Dagger and Willa chatted for a bit until Pyro came out of his office finally.

"Ah, Dagger, Hey, Sorry for making you wait so long."

"No worries, I understand."

"Congratulations on your mating."

"Thank you."

"No problem. I'm beyond happy for you. A beloved partner is the purest form of love we can have. It's a precious thing to have."

"I have adored every minute so far."

"I am pleased to hear that. Want to come to sit down in the office and we can catch up?"

"Of course."

Dagger and Pyro headed back to his office, and he closed the door once they were inside. Pyro sat in his office chair and exhaled.

"Prodigy truly knows how to be one's headache."

"Tell me about it. I've put up with him for the better part of forty years. Even now he is a pain in my backside."

"Yes, that he is. A pain."

"Did he whine to you about the fact Wick turned down his offer to work at the family company?"

"You better believe it. He was up to the ceiling with anger when I told him there was nothing I could do. Wick got to choose whatever he wanted to do."

"I was unaware that Wick had called him until this morning. I am proud of him for deciding his own path. It's best they do not work together. They don't have any kind of relationship that would be beneficial to working together."

"My thoughts were the same,"

"Prodigy needs to form a better relationship with his grandson and that will never happen if he doesn't mellow out on his entitled behavior. How is he that bad when you are not and your father wasn't that bad, either?"

"Trust me, I ask myself that when I am dealing with him. Sometimes he makes me regret my choice to wear the black robe faithfully. But then I remember how hard my father worked to restore the faith in the first family."

"Prodigy is how he is. He will have to change, eventually."

"Enough of him. Let's talk about you?"

"About me?"

"Yes, about you Dagger. What are your plans now that you have mated and your ward is through his awakening?"

"Honestly, I've thought about returning to work. Wick has his own job now and I'll be alone at home and, while, that would be good for a few days. I would get bored quickly,"

"So you have thought about my job offer, then?"

"I have. I think I would like to take you up on the offer. Though I have been out of my field for a long time, I would need some time to retrain and get back up to tip-top shape again."

"That's wonderful. We have a training area where you can train for a few weeks or months if you would like, then when you are confident you are in perfect shape again, you can take the fitness and reflex tests."

"Perfect sounds good. When did you want me to start?"

"In a couple of weeks, I'll send you a message. Until then, Spend some time with your mate, and congratulations again. I'll have Willa send you a little something on my behalf."

"Thank you."

16 - Chapter Sixteen -

Dagger spent his few free weeks spending time with Wick, and they had done plenty of things in that time. They had gone for dinners together, spent time just sitting alone in the living room watching movies, But this was far from how he had expected his last day before he went back to work to go. Wick had received a call from his grandmother, Willa. She invited them to come for dinner at her home.

Wick hadn't turned her down, even knowing that Prodigy was going to be there. Dagger didn't have a choice. He knew they expected him to be there, too. It made him slightly annoyed, but he would suck it up. They had been invited to a family function, and that was more than they normally got. Dagger would just mind his words and actions, and things should be more than fine.

Wick had dressed in a black robe, despite his distaste for them. Dagger noticed he had been wearing the black robes more and more recently. He hoped Pyro was being a positive influence. Pyro was the best one to show Wick the best things about being part of the first family.

Dagger went upstairs to his room, which had also become Wick's room in the last few weeks. He was glad he had instilled good cleaning behavior in Wick. They filled his closest beyond what it had ever been with just his own clothing. Going through the closet, he debated the black robes but settled on his white robes as he was comfortable in them.

He hoped Wick would be ok with the white robes; he didn't want Wick to be in a bad mood before going because of him.

Wick met Dagger in their bedroom and smiled softly, seeing Dagger in the white robes. He knew Dagger wouldn't be in the black ones. He was uncomfortable with them. Wick knew this. Dagger looked at Wick and gave him a smile. Dagger was almost surprised that Wick didn't ask him to change his robes.

"You look so much nicer in your white robes. The black isn't your color."

"Funny enough, you are not the only one who thinks that."

"It seems to be a consensus that a bunch of people don't like the black robes on you."

"That's fine. I'm not fond of them either."

Wick hugged Dagger suddenly and kissed his forehead.

"I'm not sure what we are walking into tonight, Dagger, I must admit. I wanted to ignore the invite, but it was from my grandmother. It didn't feel right to ignore her invite. She has always been nice to me, and to you."

"Wick, I don't care what we are walking into. We have each

other as always. That is the only thing that matters."

"Dagger, you do not know how much I appreciate everything you have done for me then and now."

"Don't worry Wick, I have some clue how much you appreciate me, I appreciate you just as much."

Dagger pecked Wick on the lips quickly before checking over his robes to make sure he was properly dressed. Dagger checked over Wick. His robe was perfectly done and Dagger smiled.

"We should head out now if we want to be there on time."

"I don't care about being late. At least I showed up," Wick said, chuckling.

"You picked that trait up right from Inn." Dagger sighed,

"Did I?"

"Yes, That man was late for everything. Everything."

"We share something else in common too, it seems."

"What would that be?"

"Our care for you."

"Wick, We don't have to talk about Inn. I know you are not fond of him and his actions."

"You're right. I am not fond of his actions, but they are what led to me being able to have you. I will not look that gift over. Trust me."

Dagger checked his watch, the one that Wick had bought him, and looked up at Wick again.

"We are going to be late."

"Fine, fine, Let's go."

He would not make them late because he decided they were ready now. Dagger could handle almost everything Wick threw at him, but like Inn, this kid aimed to make him late, all the time. Dagger never had to get used to it before because he always made sure Wick was ready well in advance, but with him being his own adult, now he couldn't.

Dagger and Wick had decided on walking to Willa's since she didn't live too far from where they did. She had bought her current house when Wick was a toddler, to come and visit more often and offer a helping hand. She saw Wick the most out of all Inn's family, Though these days she saw him less since she was working for Pyro or doing things with her other grandchildren who were younger.

Wick didn't mind that she wasn't over all the time. He enjoyed seeing her few and far in between; it made the time with her much more precious.

Dagger sighed deeply when they made it to her house. You could hear Prodigy through the open window and Wick had to lightly push Dagger up to the house with him. Wick knocked on the door and they were let inside by his uncle. He made small talk with Dagger and Wick as he let them inside.

Wick removed his shoes at the door and Dagger did the same, being careful not to dirty his white robes.

"Dagger and Wick are here."

Wick waited for Dagger to take a deep breath and compose himself before he pulled him into the sitting room. Willa smiled largely at seeing them. She hugged her grandson before hugging Dagger.

"White is such a pleasant color for you. The black of the first family really does you no justice."

"Wick said the same thing before we left."

"Of course he did."

Prodigy said hello to them both, no malice in his tone, and it caught Dagger off guard. Wick acted like it never happened. Dagger and Wick sat on the other couch across from Wick's uncle and Prodigy. Dagger kept his eyes lowered and his hands folded in his lap unless he was being spoken to. He didn't want to cause problems for Wick tonight.

Wick gently pried one of Dagger's hands from his lap and interlaced his fingers with Dagger's the whole time he maintained the conversation he was having with Prodigy. Dagger felt a little more comfortable with Wick holding his hand.

"Dagger, do you want to come to give me a hand in the kitchen?" Willa asked from the kitchen.

Dagger stood up, and Wick kissed the top of his head before letting him go to the kitchen to lend a hand.

Prodigy spoke to Wick the moment Dagger was out of earshot.

"Why is Dagger wearing his house colors and not yours? He is allowed."

"He is uncomfortable wearing the black robes. I'm sure I don't have to mention why."

"I see. Hopefully, he one day feels comfortable enough to wear them."

"I doubt that will be soon. Besides, he is more than free to wear whatever color he so chooses."

"Will Dagger and yourself be joining us for the family break?"

"I'm not sure what we will be doing. I know I have the break-off, but Dagger is going back to work and I'm not sure if he will have that time off."

"Pyro has the time off, so I'm only guessing that as a part of Pyro's guard, he would also have the time off."

"I will let you know when I find out."

Dagger returned with a tray of hot cocoa, and Willa behind him had a tray of cookies. Dagger set the tray on the table and sat down beside Wick again. Willa had told Dagger in the kitchen that Prodigy decided he was going to give a relationship with his grandson a try. Dagger would believe it when he actually saw it. He had known Prodigy enough to know that the male didn't always live up to his promises.

"Dinner will be a few more minutes before it's done, Dagger and I made snacks to help tide everyone over until then."

"Thank you for inviting us over for dinner," Dagger said,

smiling at Willa.

“Oh, It’s never a problem. You and Wick are family. You are more than welcome to come here for all the holidays. My door is always open to you two.”

“Speaking of holidays, Maybe this year Dagger and I could hold Christmas at our home. We have more than enough space for it. But you would have to mingle with the rest of our family.” Wick said, munching on a cookie.

Dagger was surprised that Wick had invited them to come for Christmas. But he further backed it up, telling them they were more than welcome at their table.

“That is a great idea, but I must ask for my own selfish needs. Are you going to hold a mating ceremony?” Willa asked, her eyes shining, almost begging for one.

“I would much like one, but that’s up to Dagger. I am down for whatever he decides he wants.”

“If you would like to have a mating ceremony, I am more than ok with that idea.”

Willa clapped her hands together, excitement filling her.

“A ceremony we will have, then. It will be the best one I’ve ever put together.”

Wick looked like he wanted to tell his grandmother no, but Dagger placed his hand on Wick’s knee and shook his head softly. Willa wanted to make it a proper event and Dagger was ok with that. After all, he knew more than anyone she wanted to to make Dagger and Inn’s marriage disappear from the family book. It wasn’t actual love.

17 - Chapter Seventeen -

Dagger headed to Pyro's office in workout attire and Pyro met him half away. Pyro was also dressed in workout attire. It mildly surprised Dagger that Pyro looked like he was also ready to work out. He didn't know Pyro even worked out.

"Hey, yeah, that outfit is perfect. You will get a bunch of uniforms, anyway."

"Sounds good. What's the plan today?"

"Practice, and training. There is plenty of time to get you back to the way you were before you took time off, though I doubt you really need the training."

"It would make me feel better."

"Hey, I don't mind, honestly. It gives you a chance to really know those you will work alongside with."

"That sounds great, thanks."

Dagger and Pyro headed to a hallway where he pulled out a

pass and held it to the door and it unlocked with a soft click.

"I have a pass for you. It's with all the uniforms."

"Alright."

"I'm quite pleased you joined my team. You know I've waited a long time for you to decide if you want to come back to your field."

"I am also quite happy I came back to work. Truth is, I've missed working, oddly enough."

"That is understandable. I think even I would miss the chaos around me if I stopped working for a long period."

"I don't regret taking the time off though lord knows I needed it, and with everything that happened, Inn and then Wick, It was a lot and I'm glad that I didn't have a job to do too."

"You have been through a lot. Now that you are on the other side, it makes you appreciate the small things you didn't do before."

"Exactly. I never realized that despite everything, I have so much."

Pyro and Dagger headed into a training room where a few people were working out. Pyro got their attention before he spoke.

"This is Dagger, House of Dagger. He is joining the ranks today. He has been out of the field for a few years, so show him what you know about working this job, get to know him and be respectful. The man is at the top of his field."

Dagger stayed quiet but looked over the five other people. He knew two of them as Pyro's personal friends and live in guards. He had met them before, but couldn't recall their names for the life of him. The other three, however, he didn't know. Pyro told the other three to go about their days like normal, and they did. His two personal guards stayed back and smiled at Dagger.

"Saxor, Laegan. I am leaving Dagger in your care. Please show him the job and where everything is. I have many meetings today."

"Got it,"

"He's safe in our hands."

Pyro left the room, leaving Dagger in the hands of his personal friends. Dagger remembered them a bit from before and a few times from Wick's childhood because Pyro and Wick were cousins and Pyro had been around a few times.

"So Dagger, this is the workout room. Showers and lockers are through this door and medical and therapy are through this door. We have many other things scattered around that are useful. Pyro set aside uniforms and a keycard for you. We are going to pick those up right now."

"Sounds good."

"Don't worry about trying to find your place to fit in. You are gold status around here. You are the best of the best."

"I don't know if I really fit that title anymore. I've been off for a long time."

"Don't worry too much about that. You have plenty of time

to get used to working again."

Dagger followed Saxor and Laegan into the locker room and got his badge and uniforms. They told Dagger it was best to make sure the tops fit, sometimes they were a little smaller than they were supposed to be. Dagger pulled his sweater off, not even thinking about where his mating mark was on him.

"Wow, Your mating mark is massive. I've never seen a mating mark that takes up so much space and it's very detailed. Is Wicks mark the same way?"

Dagger looked down at his mark that covered his whole shoulder and arm right down to the top of his hand. He had got used to being there.

"Wick's mark is on his shoulder and across a massive part of his chest. It is also very detailed. His is well hidden most times, mine not so much."

"It's beautiful. I've never seen a mark like that."

"Neither had I until I got this one."

Dagger pulled the tops and sweaters on, one after another, and they all fit very well. He slipped his sweater back on and tucked the badge into his pocket. Laegan took a call, leaving the room. Saxor just shook his head as his mate ran off, most likely to lend Pyro a hand.

"Is there anything else to see?"

"Oh yes, definitely, There is a lot here that the public doesn't get to see. A lot of the council's protection is left up to us here. Echo, Hawken and Aspen are overseeing a meeting as we speak. Laegan has probably left to go lend a hand by Pyro's order."

"You are very busy, then?"

"Eh, it honestly depends. Sometimes we are all just here training, waiting for something to do. We have a lounge room where there are books, Tv, games and a pool table. Pyro likes to make sure there is something for everyone, so if you need something, don't hesitate to let him know."

"Do I always have to wear the uniform?"

"Oh god no, we keep our uniforms here in our lockers in case we get called out. Otherwise, what you have on is pretty good. Black tights and a black sweater will be your best friend here. I would recommend a black tank top or t-shirt under the sweater too. The heat level changes all the time here."

"Yes, I've already noticed the difference in temperature everywhere we go."

"The pool room is the worst. It's kept cold as hell in there."

"Sounds pleasant."

"Feels great after training."

Saxor showed Dagger the rest of the rooms before he told Dagger he was free to head home. There really wasn't anything else for him to do today. Dagger said goodbye to Saxor and left the section they were in. Wick was waiting by the door for Dagger.

"Wick! What are you doing here?"

"I had a meeting with Pyro and he said if I wanted to wait a few more moments, you would probably be free to head home, so I waited for you."

"How did your meeting go?"

"It was long, but it went very well. How did your day go?"

"There are so many things to do here. There's a cold pool and a gym. I don't have to wear a uniform unless I'm on a job, and I know a few of the guards already. Laegan and Saxor."

"Oh, yes, Pyro's personal guards and friends."

"Yes, it seems pretty straightforward and I am positive I will enjoy this job."

"That's good. I'm thrilled to hear that."

"Grab dinner? Toast to my job and your meeting?"

"Absolutely. Where would you like to go?"

"Anywhere I don't have to get changed and can just grab dinner."

"The small food place in the market?"

"Oh yeah, That sounds perfect."

Dagger inspected Wick in his black robe and chuckled to himself. All the times he fought with that brat to get him to wear his black robes and here he was, willingly wearing them after some time. Dagger was really pleased with how much Wick had grown. They had fallen into a routine where they were happy and bonded. Dagger enjoyed it when they could have time to themselves to strengthen the bond and seek pleasure together. He also enjoyed when they just laid together in each other's company and enjoyed the simpler things.

Dagger chuckled to himself, getting Wick's attention.

"What's so funny?"

"I was just thinking about us and all this. I never once thought this would be how things had turned out. I never thought that the boy I helped raise would be my beloved partner. What's even weirder is that Prodigy seems to tolerate me more now with you than he did when I was forced with Inn. It's all just so funny to me."

"It is quite weird, isn't it? He is more pleased with me as well. It shocked me he wanted to know if we were going to spend the family week with him. I was shocked he even thought to ask that. But also he wanted to know why you didn't wear the black robes again and he even said he was hoping you would be comfortable wearing them one day."

"Willa said he was trying to connect with you finally. I honestly never expected him to actually be trying, though."

"That makes two of us."

Dagger and Wick headed off to grab dinner at the market, then head home to relax and enjoy each other's company.

18 - Chapter Eighteen -

Wick rolled over in bed, wrapping his arms around Dagger, who was still sleeping. Dagger had to get up shortly because they had plans with Willa and Prodigy for family week. All the unique members of the family had plans with them. They even had plans with Pyro and Willa at the end of the week. They were going to help them plan their ceremony. Pyro had lent them one of the nice meeting buildings for their ceremony. Pyro often lent out the building for weddings and ceremonies, so it wasn't odd for them to use the building.

"No, Let me sleep" Dagger whined, as Wick woke him up.

"I've already let you sleep in love. You have to get up now."

"You owe me big time."

"Yes, Yes, I know. Tell me what it is you want."

"A cup of coffee for a start would be nice. After that, I'll take a nice long hug and a kiss."

"Oh, yeah?"

"Yes. But again, that's just a start."

Dagger crawled out of bed only for Wick to pick him up and sling him over his shoulder. Dagger would have fought Wick's hold on him, but he was enjoying the heat that was coming from him. Wick was only dressed in pants and his chest was bare. When he put Dagger down, Dagger clung to him.

"Dagger, we need to get breakfast eaten and get dressed."

"No, You are so warm."

"You can have a few moments to hold me then, I suppose."

"You suppose?"

"Yes, We have things to do today."

Dagger sighed and hung onto Wick a little tighter. He didn't want to let him go. Dagger laid his cheek on Wick's shoulder and took a deep breath of his scent. He would have much rather just crawled back into bed with Wick and enjoyed the warmth that his partner was putting off. But he couldn't get that lucky.

"Dagger, are you ready to get ready now?"

"No."

"Dagger,"

"I'm enjoying your warmth."

"I have noticed this."

Dagger pulled away and sighed again. He just wanted to

snuggle against Wick. But they had plans, They had plans with Prodigy and Willa. That just didn't sound great to Dagger, but he wasn't about to stand them up. Groaning, he grabbed a cup of coffee and sipped it.

"Don't act like you aren't somewhat looking forward to seeing how this plays out."

"You're right, I am. If he does actually hold up to wanting a relationship with you and he manages it, then I'll be quite happy."

"And if he doesn't?"

"Then he needs to try harder. He has the chance to make this all better and have a relationship with you. Hopefully, he understands that this isn't all just up to him. At some point, even you will get sick of him not trying."

"Don't worry too much about him Dagger, it's not like this behavior of his is anything new. He has been this way since even before I was a baby. You should know this."

"Sadly, you are right, but I have some hope that he will try for you."

"Then hang onto your hope and maybe, just maybe, the fates will allow it."

"I will always have hope for you."

Wick kissed the top of Dagger's head. Wick wanted nothing more than to appease Dagger by heading back to bed. But they couldn't do that. Wick knew Dagger was still feeling the adjustment period of going back to work. Even Wick himself was good and tired after some of the long days he had. Risk made sure to let him know he would adjust to it in time. Much like Dagger would as well.

Wick felt pretty bad about having plans today after Dagger had worked a late-night shift. Dagger had insisted that he would be ok to continue with their plans last night.

Wick moved away from Dagger to make them a quick breakfast of toast and eggs. They were supposed to grab a meal and some other things with Prodigy and Willa. So he didn't want to fill Dagger up with food.

After Wick dressed and made sure he got Dagger dressed, he called for a shuttle and they made their way over to Prodigy's home. Wick had got his way because Dagger was tired enough he didn't fight him about the black robe he dressed him in.

At Prodigy's, Wick didn't even knock, he just let himself in. Dagger wanted to give him trouble for it, but there was no point. Prodigy would not get the door for them, anyway.

Dagger and Wick could hear Prodigy speaking from the sitting room. Once they slipped their shoes off, that was where they headed. Wick pulled Dagger close, tucking him against his side, right before they entered the room. Wick wasn't trying to prove anything to anyone in that room, he just thought Dagger might be more comfortable being this close in this house.

The smiling face of his grandmother made Wick smile, too.

"Good morning, happy family week."

"Morning, happy family week to you, too."

Dagger just nodded his head softly. He didn't want to speak because he was sure he would just start yawning. Willa looked at Dagger and sighed.

"You never know enough to call when you are at your limit, do you, Dagger? I know you were working till two this morning. You should still be in bed."

Dagger went to answer, but Prodigy spoke too.

"You should have moved our plans, or canceled them."

"I asked him last night if he could do all this today and he insisted he would."

"I am more than fine, thank you. It is not the first time, nor will it be the last time. But we had plans and we will stick to them." Dagger said, yawning as soon as he finished speaking.

Wick pulled Dagger behind him as they went to sit down on one of the three couches. Wick knew how tired Dagger was. He could feel it. He felt slightly bad for waking his lover up and making him come to his grandfathers. Dagger had been the one to insist he could do it.

"We are heading out for lunch. Is there anything you two would prefer?"

"There is a really nice place Dagger and I go to at the market. We could also do some shopping," Wick said softly.

"Oh, I know where you're talking, The place with the fantastic sandwiches!"

"Yes, that place."

Dagger nodded along with Wick's recommendation.

"What should we do after that? There are all kinds of festivals going on today."

"There are firework shows all week, but the opening night is always the largest one." Prodigy said matter-of-factly.

"Prodigy is right. The fireworks tonight are the best until the end of the week." Dagger said, looking at Wick and shrugging.

"Dagger, you will hardly make it dark. You are exhausted," Wick said, pulling Dagger even closer to him than before.

"It would be worth it, even if I am running on low sleep."

They chatted for a few more minutes before Prodigy suggested they go get lunch. Wick and Dagger agreed. Prodigy called for a shuttle to take them to the front of the market. He did so that Dagger, who was already wiped out, didn't have to worry about walking.

Getting into the shuttle, Dagger laid his head on Wick's shoulder and listened to his conversation with Prodigy. The conversation had to do with their ceremony that was in the works of being planned. Prodigy offered some help in planning and helping to pay for it. Wick turned him down on the offer, however. Dagger wanted to tell Wick not to be so quick to turn him down, but Wick quickly explained why.

"It's not that I don't want your help, but I want to pay for everything. I don't even want Dagger to help. Dagger has paid for my entire upbringing. I want to pay for the things he wants now. The mating ceremony is only the start."

"That is honorable Wick." Prodigy said, almost complimenting him.

"He's a good kid." Dagger mumbled against Wick's shoulder, mostly asleep.

When they arrived at the market, Wick woke Dagger up and fixed his hair before leading him into the market for lunch. Dagger had a little more wind in him now. The few minutes of the nap in the car gave him a touch of energy.

Dagger decided he would get a cup of coffee to help keep him awake when they ordered lunch. Dagger sipped his coffee and felt like he was coming back from the dead again. Once lunch arrived on the table, for once they talked and had a conversation, Something Prodigy had never done before with Dagger. He had always fallen into silence over meals when it was Inn and him.

Dagger engaged in the conversation and kept up with what they were talking about once he was fully caffeinated and sure he would not pass out on the spot again.

After lunch, they wandered around the market for hours, until the sun set. Prodigy and Willa had left Dagger and Wick to wander around the market by their own choice. Now they planned to sit in the grass and watch the fireworks ending the first day of the family week. It had gone well for them too, never had things gone that well for them.

As the first fireworks touched the sky, it was Wick who spoke through the bangs and flashes of colors.

"I think I would like the mating ceremony as soon as possible, hell even tomorrow would be ok. We need nothing fancy, just you and me and our families as witnesses. I want our houses to be lined from now until the end of time."

"I also want that." Dagger whispered into the cooling air of the night. He brought Wicks' lips to his and kissed him. The surrounding fireworks loudly go off and give a little more light to see each other's faces. The shame Dagger felt about a lot of things seemed to melt away then. None of it mattered. Wick was all that mattered to him.

19 - Chapter Nineteen -

Dagger and Wick made their bonding completely official by applying for a house title together, something they had neglected to do until then. Dagger became Dagger, House of Wick, house of Black, First family. Dagger felt wrong in the black robes but didn't make a fuss about them since he was more than allowed to wear them again. In those who believed in marriage after matings eyes, they were officially married now, but Wick and Dagger had chosen for the future to actually get married the human way. Better known as a mating ceremony in Skorwn terms.

They were celebrating an imperial holiday with Wick's grandmother Willa. She was the Ex-Wife of Prodigy, Mother of all his children, and she had a soft spot for Dagger and her grandson. She always had. She was just that way.

They had started to plan a mating ceremony but got busy with work and just life around them, so the plans had fallen into the background. Wick thought about it and thought about it until at last, he couldn't just think about it any longer. He had to do something. He had gone out and picked the perfect ring for Dagger without him catching on. Wick had also invited Risk to join them for dinner without Dagger knowing. So when he showed up, Wick felt the fire under his rear to ask Dagger. Wick had put the ring under the metal plate cover and he was currently taking it to the table. Setting it in front of Dagger, he watched Dagger question the lid. He knew this is what Dagger would do, since it was something they had never really used at all.

"Dagger, you are cutting the chicken. I ruin it every time. I would hate to ruin it tonight, too." He hissed.

"Alright, I understand. I'll do it." Dagger said softly, Smiling at his beloved partner.

When Dagger opened the lid, his heart stood still. The gold band sparkled even in the bit of light in the dining room. He closed the lid and turned to find Wick on one knee. Dagger couldn't think of anything else but the horrible words that slipped from his mouth at the moment.

"Holy shit!"

"Dagger, that's hardly appropriate." Risk said, laughing. He was excited for the two of them to start this chapter of their lives like this.

Looking at Wick, Dagger started to cry. He really had cried little ever in his life. There had been moments. But they were few and far apart.

"Dagger, I've loved you since the moment you held me as an infant. It would be the best moment of my life, besides the night we became bonded if you would marry me."

"Of course. Or I do, Or yes. Anything that means I will

marry you."

Wick took the ring out of the open box and slipped it on Dagger's finger, kissing him softly. The ring stood out beautifully from his males bonding mark. They all sat around the table and true to word Dagger cut the chicken so Wick couldn't murder the meat. They used gold and silver for solely mating ceremony based robes and those of the council.

Wick knew Dagger had worn black last time. He had seen the robe. But this time Dagger got married, Wick wanted to see him covered in gold, right down to his robe. The gold would complement Dagger and his looks thoroughly.

After dinner Risk had left because he had business to deal with, but Willa stayed because she wanted to talk about the wedding. She was really excited to be helpful again. Dagger could remember when he married Inn the thoughts made him sad for a moment and he thought about his long since passed friend. Dagger wondered if Inn would support the idea of Dagger getting married to his only son, the one he had raised. At the moment, Dagger cared little. He was happy with Wick, and they were beloved partners. No one could stop this.

Dagger also thought about Willa, who was more involved now than she was before. She hadn't been there because she didn't support the idea of basically selling off her son. She had been against the idea and had made that known in the beginning and right until just before Inn lost his life. But, It wasn't like she didn't like Dagger because she had been in their home after the wedding and they got along perfectly. It was just the idea of what Prodigy had done with their youngest son's future she couldn't stand. Willa stood up, Offering to help Wick take the dishes to the kitchen.

She returned after setting the dishes on the counter and looked at Dagger, her eyes holding nothing but love and appreciation for him.

"I prefer this match. Much better than your first, Dagger, Son of Risk. Inn was a good kid, but not your match. It shouldn't have happened, but I won't make either of us relive that horror. I am just happy there is a way forward for you and everything you gave up for my son and his mistakes."

"Thank you. That means so much coming from you, Willa. But, I don't regret Inn however, I was happy I could make his life a little easier until his sad departure from this world."

"You two actually suit each other well. But your bonding marks are proof enough of that. I look forward to seeing how much you two grow together. You have a lot of promise to be a strong and influential couple in our society."

Both Dagger and Wick at that moment had the same thought about how right she was. They were suited for each other. There was much they wanted to do together in the future.

"I also look forward to seeing if you two adopt any wards to share in your house. You both have a lot to offer children, much like Wick himself."

"I wouldn't mind some children, but in a few years, Dagger has only just got rid of his own ward." Wick snickered, rubbing Dagger's back.

"I wouldn't mind another one or two, but in a few years, I want to get back into work and have some time with just Wick and me as a couple."

"That's understandable. You just returned to work and Wick

just started his job. I think that's a pretty good plan. Besides your brother's have enough children for you to spoil right now."

"Yes, Two new babies. My brothers have had the new baby field covered for at least ten years. I had Wick, then they popped out one every few years. If they don't knock it off, there will be too many of us from the House of white, descendants of Risk. There are enough of us now."

"Please, there isn't enough of your family line."

"That's what you think. My father is lucky he doesn't have more grandchildren now, hell the man will be broke before he hits five centuries if my brothers keep it up."

"I have just a few grandchildren and that's how I like it," Willa said, looking at Wick with love in her eyes.

"I was the first grandchild, and that is all I care about," Wick said teasingly.

"You are also the one your grandfather thinks is a pest. I wouldn't be too pleased about that," Willa said, teasing him back.

"Yes, But I am an adult pest. The only adult of his grandchildren. There are things he can do with me. He can't do anything with the others. Makes me special."

"Wick. That man just started having dinner with you. Don't get your hopes up, he will take you for grandfather and grandson days." Willa said, annoyed with the behavior of her ex-husband.

"That man is going to be so out of tune when he finally gets a beloved partner of his own. If he even believes in that kind of thing." Wick said sharply.

"Wick, be nice. Maybe that's just what he needs to make himself a little less sharp towards others."

"It might make him worse, though."

"Only the fates know what is in the cards for your grandfather. Until then, we can only hope he changes himself for the better."

Dagger and Willa chatted for a while more. While Wick cleaned up the kitchen. Dagger looked at the ring on his hand. It made his hand feel weird, but he loved the look of it. Dagger suddenly remembered that Wick was ready to just throw it all over and get married on a whim. He tapped his chin once before looking at Willa.

"How do you feel about next weekend?"

"For?" She said, raising her eyebrow.

"A mating ceremony."

"I hear it's supposed to be a lovely sunny day, with a chance of rain at night, perfect for a mating ceremony."

"Hope you are not busy, then."

"Seems I will be. I have a mating ceremony to officiate for my grandson and his beloved partner."

20 - Chapter Twenty -

They dressed Dagger in gold just like Wick had suggested, But added some black touches here and there to show the family he was joining. The mood at this wedding was much lighter than the one where he married Inn. Everyone actually looked like they wanted to be there, not anywhere but there. Still, he compared Wick to Inn. He wasn't sure if he was trying to prove that they were so different or if he was trying to prove if Wick was even Inn's son. Pushing the thought of Inn away, he told himself he was thinking of the past. This was where his true future began. Wick was his true future, the one thing he waited forever for. All that would begin now, from this moment forward. It was only the weekend after they had got engaged, but Dagger truly knew his partner and future husband better than he thought. He still learned things about Wick every day that he hadn't known before. Like the way, his nose wrinkles when he leaves the drapes open to see the moon, and the sunlight hits his face in the morning. It was little things like that that Dagger really enjoyed finding out about his lover. Dagger was more than ready to make Wick his forever. There was no doubt in his heart that this wasn't what he wanted. He wanted him for better; he had for worse.

The wedding music started and Dagger was going to walk up the aisle. It wasn't the normal way to do it, but the couple preferred to do it this way. It gave no one the title of the female in the relationship. They were equals and there was no missing that here. They were both powerful males who each brought their strengths to the pairing.

Willa had offered to be the witness for their marriage after Dagger had asked her. Standing at the front, she watched the males walking down the aisle. They linked their elbows as they made the walk. They were perfect besides each other. The enormous frame of her grandson fit in well with the lean frame of Dagger. She smiled, the family book weighing heavily on her hands. This book was a book of all the weddings in the bloodline, and she treasured it deeply. Willa had whited out the line where Dagger and Inn's name once sat wrongfully. It gave her great pleasure to remove it, too. She was happy to watch them sign the book.

Willa spoke the moment they reached the platform, turning to face each other. The joy she felt was immense, and she knew this was a good pairing.

"Males of the Skorwn, Females of the Skorwn, houses of all cloth, we join in the wedding of Dagger, house of Wick, cloth of white and Wick, House of Wick, Cloth of black.

Does anyone interrupt the proceedings to halt peace for the joining?"

Moments ticked by as Willa waited for someone to say something, but not one of the hundred people in attendance spoke, They knew no one would. There were many who looked forward to this proper joining. Willa started to speak again.

"Dagger, Son of Risk. What words do you have to offer up to Wick, Ward of Dagger, Son of Inn, Treasured child of Risk?"

"Wick, I have known you since you were a newborn. You were always so much more than just the son of my loss. I put so much into helping you become the male you are, but you exceeded the limits I wished for you. When you became my beloved partner, I knew we would end up here, and I knew from that day you would have my hand, heart, and soul. If you would take me as I am, I will be the faithful husband and friend you look for from here, until the last breath I take in this world and the next."

"Do you take Dagger, Son of Risk, for what he offers?"

"I do."

Willa saw the males smile at each other deeper than she had seen from them before. This was so pleasing to her. They both were going to be happy and healthy, the only things she wanted for them both. They deserved it.

"Wick, Son of Inn, Treasured child of Risk."

"Dagger, There are many words I would say if I could put them together properly, and I wish I could, but they escape me when I look into your eyes. All I can say is when my father gave you me, you took a chance on me knowing I could lash out or be difficult, but you held true. You gave me everything you had then and now. You gave me a family, a father, a best friend, someone I could share my every moment with. I will give you all I can offer and all I can offer is a chance at happiness and hope you will stay as I grow and change further. My hope is alongside you."

"Do you take Wick, son of Inn, Treasured child of Risk, for what he offers?"

"I do, from now until my last immortal breath,"

Willa watched as they gave each other their rings, and then she spoke again.

"You two males may kiss and join forevermore."

She watched them share a kiss before she laid the book out on the table with the pen and pin. They signed the book in the blood of their now married bodies.

They signed the book right over the white-out piece of the page. Dagger knew exactly where he had signed. His name sat above where his name had been the last time, but this time it held so much more worth. Wick's name sat nicely over his father's and he didn't even feel bad for doing it. If anything, it made him feel pleased.

Wick pulled Dagger against his chest then and held him there. It was all real Dagger was his husband at last. Wick was pleased with the robe Dagger was in. It looked beautiful on him, but didn't make him look feminine. It brought out all his handsome features. Willa had painted along some of the parts of Dagger's mating mark with gold paint.

Wick looked into Dagger's eyes one last time before he kissed his husband, as he had never kissed him before. They were joined in mind, body and soul now. For all of their shared forever.

Cheering was heard as Pyro flexed some of his powers for amazing effects. Wick leaned down and whispered into Dagger's ear.

"If this is all I get in life, I would do it a thousand times over."

Dagger was feeling emotional again. He had to turn away from Wick so the male didn't see the tears brimming in his eyes and running down his face. Happiness was plentiful inside of him, for the first time in a really long time. He was trying to pull it all together. There was still cake and dinner and a whole reception to get through yet.

"Dagger, My love, We can step outside for a few minutes if you need to get some air and process all your emotions."

"I would very much like that. I need to take it all in. But you need to come with me, too. I need to be held by you. Alone, for just a few moments."

"I would love to just hold you alone for a few moments."

They snuck out the back and into the dark of the outside. Wick pulled Dagger towards him and into his arms. He took a deep breath and enjoyed the scent of his now husband. His forever was brighter than ever.

"Dagger, If my father could see any moment of my life, I want to be this one."

"How come?" Dagger muttered into Wick's chest.

"My father would know that we are both happy and healthy, and well taken care of. I'm sure that is all he would want."

"I agree. I hope the fates allow him to see this moment, maybe even live in this moment."

They stayed there until Risk, and Willa came to check on them. They stayed back at first, just watching Wick and Dagger. Then they crashed their delicate moment to drag them back inside for dinner and cake. There was still a dance they had to complete too, and then family wedding photos.

Risk took Dagger's hand and spoke.

"I'm so damn proud of you. Words escape me the moment I need them most."

Willa took Wick inside, where his uncle and the rest of them congratulated him. But it all felt empty without his husband beside him. He knew Risk was having a private moment with him.

When Dagger was returned to the ceremony, he was in something less flashy and more comfortable and as much as Wick enjoyed it, he liked him dressed up as the man he had fallen for. He took his husband's hands and brought them to his lips, kissing them.

"You are just the person I was looking to spend my forever with."

"I was just thinking something identical. Funny how we think alike."

Thank you

Thank you for checking out 'House of Dagger'. You can leave me an honest review of my work on Amazon.

Check back for new books!

Manufactured by Amazon.ca
Bolton, ON

28157024R00090